THE CELL BLOCK PRESENTS...

PRETTY GIRLS LOVE

BAD BOYS

THE PRISONER'S GUIDE TO GETTING GIRLS

Published by: THE CELL BLOCK™

THE CELL BLOCK
P.O. Box 1025
Rancho Cordova, CA 95741

Website: thecellblock.net
Facebook/thecellblockofficial
Instagram: @mikeenemigo

Cover design by Mike Enemigo

Send comments, reviews, or other business inquiries:
thecellblock.net@mail.com
Visit our website: thecellblock.net

INTRO

First of all, I want to thank everyone who has been supporting The Cell Block. It's because of you why we're able to continue to put out these urban novels, resource guides and self-help books. Real has got to recognize real because from the inside of our level IV cells we've been putting out content that's been bought and sold from coast to coast!

For those of you who read my How to Hustle and Win book, you pretty much know how me and Mike Enemigo hooked up. You read about how I got out and moved to the Virgin Islands. I actually sent my manuscripts back into prison (from the streets) to get published. Usually, it's the other way around, so that alone gotta tell you that I knew I was fucking with a real goon.

To make a long story extremely short, cold case detectives came back with more evidence and they came and got me again! Yeah, bullshit... But it's good, though, I came in knowing what to expect. Knowing my potential and understanding that no matter where I'm at, time is money, has kept me sane. I don't care if I'm sitting in a trap in Chattanooga, a condo on Clearwater Beach, or working off that burner phone in Sacramento, I refuse to sit idle. I refuse to stand still and grow stagnate. That's called work ethic and it shows in everything I do.

This book, in true Cell Block fashion, is for the block

bleeders who are behind enemy lines. It's for MAC's who are used to getting what they want when they want it. This guide for getting women is for all of you who get up every morning, roll up them mattresses and will the universe to manifest something out of nothing.

In the following pages you're gonna find poems, love songs, intro letters, and real tried and true game that you can use to crack any female you come in contact with while incarcerated. Now, based on the strict censorship in a number of Southern states I'm forced to pick and choose my words carefully, or else risk your mailroom turning back this book. So read between the lines when I say I'm giving you the knowledge on how to seduce any female you come in contact with while you're incarcerated. This book isn't just about pen pals!

This book isn't for "inmates" either. This book is for "convicts." If you don't know the difference between the two, then chances are, you're an inmate. If you're an inmate and you just ordered this book you'll most likely take it one of two ways:

1. You won't believe you're capable of accomplishing what I say you can because you've never seen anyone else do it. Therefore, you won't give it your all and you'll remain a square.

OR

2. Your eyes will be opened to a whole other realm of prison life that you never thought was possible. You'll learn the lessons and use them and get them all the way up! It's on you! Game is to be sold, not told. You bought the book so now it's on you to take your time and learn its lessons.

$$\$\$\$\$\$\$$$

Prison is what you make it. The decisions you make today will dictate how you're living tomorrow. If you're content with either depending on your grandmother or mother to look out for you, and you don't care about the financial/emotional strain your incarceration is putting on them – then there is no need to keep reading. But, if you're either tired of being broke, or just want to live above your means, then this book is definitely for you.

Anyone who's been to prison has learned that without some sort of support from the streets, accomplishing anything of substance is next to impossible. Having a support network on the streets can mean the difference between going to sleep hungry at night, getting out early, or doing hard time without visits and mail. In other words, with a support system on the outside, your prison time can be a lot easier. This book will walk you through the steps of creating a support network from scratch.

If you want to go to the store on every draw, make phone calls every day, get mail every day, hit them visits every weekend, get phones, "work" and/or everything else that defines penitentiary rich – I can get you there. All I ask is that you take the lessons in this book seriously and believe in yourself. You are capable of shaping the world around you.

And let's face it; you're gonna need a female on your team. Any which way you look at it, the only way you're gonna get where you need to go is if you got a Becky that's ready to run for you. Sometimes you'll need four or five Beckys... it's all up to you.

That's what this book is all about. So if you're ready to tip the scales of justice in your favor – let's get to work.

CHAPTER ONE
END GAME

I think the first mistake most people make when setting goals is that they start out without an end game. You may "think" you've got an end game, but once you reach the finish line you realize that had you been more prepared you would've been able to fully capitalize off of all the opportunities that were opened once you embarked on your mission.

I know this because I've been there and done that. I can literally write a whole book just based on the blunders I've made with women. It's like that old saying, "You never know what you have until you lose it." In the pen pal game, you miss opportunities when you go into it without an end game.

First of all, we need to point out the fact that if you're looking for a pen pal, you're most likely in prison. Since you're incarcerated, you're goals for obtaining women are different than they would be on the street. In the free world the main goal in meeting women is sex. Real talk; whether it's in the forefront of your mind, or in the subconscious, 99% of time there is a thought of warm, wet pussy posted up in the corner of your mind whenever you approach a female you don't know.

Well... I hate to tell ya' the bad news, but you can't live off of pussy in prison. Not if you're trying to reach above and beyond the boundaries the government has set up for you. And along with pussy, I have to talk about love… Man, this is a TCB production. If you have read any other book on the line–up then you already know there's no love in the game. We're real MAC's, real Players, real Gangstaz. The game don't stop just 'cuz we got caught by the cops.

So let's stop beating around the proverbial bush: You don't need pussy and you don't need love. All that shit is superficial. What you need is absolute devotion! I don't care how old she is, what race she is, how much experience she has, or how many guys are chasing her; my end game is to obtain total, undying devotion from every woman I set my sights on.

And what I mean by total devotion is that, from the inside of my prison cell, I can make her (willingly) change all her plans in life to mentally, physically and financially support me throughout my whole time in prison. I want her to be willing to go to ridiculous lengths to make me comfortable in prison. I want to have priority over everything in her life including her family. That's my end game. If it's not yours then you need to put this book down right now!

If you want to meet a female while you're in prison who'll run for you, send letters, send money, accept your calls, run your social media, come visit you, buy you a phone… then this book will give you the game to get all that and more.

In this section we'll start out with the basics. The first thing you need to do is put yourself out there. In a later part of this book we'll build on face–to–face game so you can work on females who you see and meet around you, but right now let's start with the pen pals.

Getting an ad on the right website is first and foremost. Personally, most of my luck has come from WriteAPrisoner.com. I like their set–up because someone can send you and email straight through them after seeing your profile, and W.A.P. will 3–way that message to you. I seriously recommend that company because I've seen and experienced positive results from them.

Nevertheless, that doesn't mean there aren't other websites or organizations out there that work just as well. There are, you just gotta ask around and find out where the guys at your prison are getting the most hits from.

There are websites out there where you post free bio's, and those work too. But just remember this: In this life, you get what you pay for. Another thing: If you're serious about making your life in prison better, you have to be willing to make sacrifices.

A lot of these places accept stamps as payment for their services. We all know that stamps are used as currency on most prison yards. Even if you don't have someone who will give you the forty or fifty dollars that it'll take to get your profile started, it doesn't mean you can't hustle it up yourself!

I know a guy whose homeboy (from the streets) told him that he had forty dollars for him. That he could send him the money to his commissary account, or he could send that forty to a pen pal website. This meant the convict had a choice to make; either put an ad on a website and go hungry that month, or order some soups and chips and worry about the pen pal thing later. The convict told his homey to send the money to the pen pal company. He didn't get any meaningful replies until 9 months later, but when he did get that 1 hit he made the best of it and he eventually married that woman who had contacted him. Real talk; real story; real shit!

That's what I mean when I say that you gotta be willing to make sacrifices! He went hungry for a month, and that shit didn't pay off for 9 months. Even after he first met ol' girl, she still didn't break bread for a while, but when it was all said and done, he was getting conjugal visits and all that.

Throughout the next few pages I've added a few bios that I found in the classified section of a newspaper I read. There were a lot more than the ones I've listed, but I chose these because I think they are well written.

Writing bio's can be tricky at times since you're limited to the amount of space and you're competing with others. A philosophy I like to use is of a used car salesman. When you're trying to sell a car, you never wanna tell the buyer about every single dent or ding. You want to point out all the good shit like air conditioning, fresh paint, interior, new exhaust pipes... Same thing with your bio. It always helps to list your accomplishments and goals. You're trying to sell yourself so it helps if you verbally dress yourself up to create the image of a diamond in the rough, or knight in shining armor.

I've added these bio's for you to go through and take out the best lines to create your own. You can also use them as reference for inspiration, or completely copy them. Whatever works for you.

You are the lord and master of your own universe. You make the rules. Scan through each one and decide what best fits your swagger. Then send it in to whatever pen pal website you choose and watch how many fish start biting...

BIO's

Black/Indian male, single, 6'2", 195 lbs, athletically built, light golden brown skin complexion, brown eyes. I love to play sports and stay fit. I also love to read and write poetry. Nevertheless, I am not complicated, just in search of an open–minded, straight–forward, down–to–earth female. One who is above and beyond the artificial role plays and emotional games. If you're out there, Your Highness, I would love to politic with you on a level of love and friendship. I promise to answer all letters and send photos to the heart that is sincere. So get at me ASAP!

$$$$$

I'm sincerely searching for the precious treasures of your loving heart and extraordinary soul which is the unique mystery that is untold. We can astronomically travel beyond the moon and start to mend your broken heart and heal your emotional scars. I truly want to explore the unique beauty of your precious mind and I assure you that you will be overwhelmingly fascinated within mine. Let us crystalize what you've fantasized and the exquisite reality of our precious relationship will materialize love, loyalty, affection, compassion, communication and understanding is a must. So let's start sincerely building our divine foundation on trust.

$$$$$

SBM who believes that strangers are nothing but friends who haven't met yet, so there's no need to be alarmed. I'm not the type to play games. I am the type to keep it real.
If I ever felt I had to be fake in order to be accepted by you then I would rather stay real and lose your friendship because that would be a small price to pay for a worthy cause. So if you're tired of short commercials of pain, tragedies and confusions and are ready for respect, compassion and companionship, then contact me and let's go from there.

$$$$$

185 lbs., 6'1", open–minded, fun–loving individual with intelligent conversation combined with a passion for music, art and all forms of beauty. I'm currently looking for that individual who deserves to be individually spoiled, pampered and reassured; someone who's not intimidated by affection and appreciation. I guess you can say I'm looking for that exotic rose among the adequate flowers, someone who believes in loyalty and isn't stagnated by insecurities or infatuated with childhood games but ready to meet me on an intellectual level and create something worth embracing. I'm an individual who finds pleasure in socializing, networking and establishing solid foundations. All are encouraged to write, no matter what age, creed, or gender.

$$$$$

I'm 28 yrs old, 6'2", 196 lbs, brown eyes with brushed waves. I got a pretty boy, bad guy, smart dude swag. I'm from Akron, OH, but love to travel. I'm spontaneous, outgoing, open–minded, funny, cocky, confident and an inch away from

9

conceited. I'm one who believes that common interests and familiar grounds are a great place to build an empire for an impeccable friendship. With that being said, I'm looking for someone who mirrors my character. If this female is you I'll be waiting to hear from you because this ad is for you.

$$$$$

Are you woman enough to accept the thoughts of a man who has been captive for years? So many years in fact he kneels to embrace each tear that falls from your flawless face. Are you woman enough to see with your sparkling eyes beyond the torment and mental scars that molded the presence of my life? Are you woman enough to see with your mind's eye that I may not be the rapist, the molester, or the one who shot that innocent kid? In fact, I could be just the man that you need, one who did what he thought was just, just to see that his child could eat. Are you woman enough to feel with your heart the parts of this cold steel cage, the cuffs and the scuffs from billy–clubs and the infant meals that are spilled on the trays to erase the strength of a race? Are you woman enough to erase my faults and embrace a man who would do it all again simply because he loves you? If you are the one, then I'm here waiting for you.

$$$$$

32 yrs old from Dallas, TX. My hobbies include reading, sports (any), dancing (which I think I can get down), writing, cooking and really anything physical. I am very easy going and a communicative person. I am an optimist and love making people laugh. I'm very social, adventurous, friendly, and amiable and I know how to hold a conversation of substance. I am a very spiritual person and love children, seeing that I have none of my own. I value friendship and I

place loyalty above or in high regard. I love music which includes all kinds of country, rock, rap, alternative, jazz, blues. Looking for genuine friendship.

$$$$$

Make a quantum leap! Potential and possibilities for greatness are here to grasp the space afforded to personal description is too small to capture and convey my being. To try would be superficial because I'm multi–layered, more substance than sizzle. So here is what I will give you: Mature, 44 yrs old, heterosexual, African American male seeking correspondence with progressive people who don't settle for anything less than they deserve in all areas of life. If that's you, intrigue and candor awaits you.

$$$$$

SBM, 51 yrs old, in search of someone to shed a little light on these grey walls and in return I'd be willing to share my desires for the future. My incarceration is only temporary. However, this new journey that I've chosen comes with a new thirst for life, knowledge and companionship. One of the world's most sought after secrets is happiness. I realize that happiness comes in many forms. The happiness I seek comes in the form of a letter. Words are powerful. Words can be a new beginning for a person. Certain things in life are inevitable, like we know that the sun will rise and set with each day! I can only hope that our chance of meeting will be an inevitable moment. So I hope the mailman will pick up and deliver your first letter to me...

$$$$$

BM, 35, 5'9", 175 lbs. I'm sending this message in a bottle as if I were stranded on a deserted island hoping it doesn't fall on deaf ears. I'm in need of someone open to building an intimate friendship. Besides my daughters, what I miss the most is the touch of a woman. Deeper appreciation of womanhood is a hard lesson I feel on a regular basis. If I have managed to pique your interest, please pursue your curiosity.

$$$$$

The greatest diamonds are products of enduring the greatest pressures. I'm a 36 y/o black man. I'm seeking to raise the interest to write me from 3 types:

1.I'd love to hear from a Muslima.

2.From politically active individuals and organizations.

3.From an explorative woman who would take a venture with a trusted man temporarily confined to a land where there are few.
I enjoy both the simplicity and complexity of life. I'm a straight–forward speaker and progressive thinker. Most descriptive of me is that I am genuine in all that I say and do. Write to me at...

$$$$$

ATTN: Voluptuous black woman. Are you tired of the same old game run by guys who know what you want to hear but aren't prepared to give you the attention, or appreciation you deserve? If you have the time and patience to wait this year out while getting to know me, I promise you I'll commit the time it'll take to get to know you... give you the prompt reply and be that shoulder you can lean on.

$$$$$

In the spirit of humanity, allow these words to inspire a dialogue designed to enhance each other's lives. I'm a 45 year old brotha with a vintage swagg, who embodies all the positive attributes of a man. The gift and curse of incarceration has redefined my concept and my role as a man. I'm currently housed in a prison, trapped in thought and seeking a friend to release the pressure of boredom. I'm non-judgmental, good for   uplifting conversations and perhaps a laugh or two. If you're looking for a potential friend you've already found one in me...

CHAPTER TWO

LETTERS

I'm gonna start this chapter out by letting you know a little secret: There's different levels to this shit, bruh. This book isn't just about getting pen pals to write you and send you money. However, since we're in prison, some of your opportunities to pull females will depend on your pen game. With that in mind, I've added over 30 prewritten letters for you to browse and use, or chop and screw to fit whatever situation you're in.

Before we get to them I wanna break down certain aspects about the female thought process (psychology) so that you can understand why they seem to act so differently than men. Maybe, after reading what I got to say you'll be able to view these letters from an optimal vista.

The first thing that most guys get wrong is that they tend to label all women in a category called "emotional creatures." If you ask any man what the difference between men and women is, they'll immediately tell you that women are more emotional.

That's bullshit! That's a blanket statement used by men who have never spent enough time with different women to really understand them. If you've ever spent quality time in the presence of a Boss Bitch you'd know that women are extremely calculating and analytical. Their only differences from us are biological and physical. And it's because of these differences that they have been forced to adopt unique survival strategies.

We all know that women are physically smaller and weaker than men. This plus the fact that they play different roles in the mating process have forced them to adopt different psychological strategies for surviving. It's all extremely logical, but it's deep, so if you're a "basic" individual I don't expect you to be up on this type of knowledge, wisdom or understanding.

If you are quick to give up when a woman does something you don't understand you'll never get far in your pursuit for pussy and power. Labeling them as all being emotional is a copout. It's lazy, and it's a sign of ignorance because you're not realizing that most of the things people do or say are often far below our conscious awareness.

When guys approach females, whether through the mail, phone or in person, sometimes things don't work out because the level of wisdom she's working with. While guys are spending their time checking out a girl's tits and ass, she's breaking down his whole delivery: His demeanor, his swagger, his aura... all this tells her if he's a winner or not. Now, how can you tell me that that thought process is one of an emotional creature?

There is one major difference between men and women that deserves to be noted at this juncture: Men are wired to pursue status, to elevate their status. Rims, jewelry, clothes and money— all that shit we were chasing on the streets all had an underlying connection... status! For women, status isn't as important as interconnection. Females have the same level of drive as we do, only it's not for status, it's for interconnection.

[Interconnection: to connect with one another]

Interconnections are how they identify themselves. For a female, her level of self–esteem is based on the number and quality of connections she has with other people. And one thing that's interesting is that when women get caught up in the man's game of pursuing status, they end up performing better than men for a number of reasons. One of the main reasons is their ability to interact with other people effectively.

Women are no less illogical or irrational than men, they just have a different survival strategy. It also holds true that men are no less emotional than women; we process those emotions differently, we experience them differently. They have more empathy than us. When one of their friends tell them about a problem they know how to be there for comfort purposes. What we do is try to come up with a solution, totally ignoring the internal aspects of said conflicts.

In my book How to Hustle and Win: Sex, Money, Murder Edition I explained the fact that humans are social creatures. On a psychological level, the highest need that we all strive to meet is self–actualization: where we feel like as an individual, I feel like I am the person that I want to be.

For men, that actualization might come in the eyes of our peers when we hit the block on new rims and paint. For women, a simple compliment like "thank you, what you're doing for me means a lot" means the world to her.

This is why you must be conscious of what comes out your pen when you're scribing to a female. What may seem as trivial or repetitive to us may be just what baby needs to read when she rips open that envelope.

Throughout the next few pages there are standardized letters that you can remix to tailor your specific needs. You may only use a paragraph out of a letter to compliment your own game— that's cool. Do you, but do it to win!

LETTERS

Dear Name,

How ya' doing? I wanna start by telling you that I like

and appreciate your forwardness and honesty. As I read your missive I started smiling about some of your statements and the way you responded to some of the things that I covered in my letter. My intuition tells me that you're the type of person that I can get along with and that's refreshing to think about.

I felt like I know you. Of course, I'm not saying that I really know you, but yeah, I know you. We're cut from the same cloth. Through your letter I can sense your presence. You're a Boss!

Listen; (name), let's take this one step at a time. There's no need to rush. I'm not about to make any demands or ask for any commitments. Just knowing you is what's up!

Now, you're probably thinking "this guy is just spittin' game." And if that's the case, I don't fault you for being real. I like you. I can truly see myself spending lots and lots of time with you. Mostly because you're sharp and insightful. I like that in a woman.

I hope that through our letters with one another, we'll get the chance to learn things about each other. For instance, the way to spot a bullshitter is to watch his actions very closely and pay very little mind to what comes from his mouth or pen. I know the stereotypes that people give prisoners. And I'm always so gutta with people that they just automatically think it has to be a con. But if nothing is asked of you, where are the games being played?

(Name), I've done enough partying to last a lifetime. All of my thoughts now revolve around finding that special person to share the rest of my life with. Children? There isn't any room for kids. My lady will be my child. All of my time and love is only to be focused on her. I love children, so don't misinterpret where I'm coming from, but I want to spoil my woman. And I promise that you'll never get bored with me. I have the power to keep a smile on your face forever if I choose to do so. Bragging? Naw, I just know what I'm capable of.

Most people go their whole life with another person and

never really get to know her. I want to know you. I mean really know you!! Communication is one of the keys to a successful relationship. I don't want to second guess what my woman may be thinking. I want a closeness that defies gravity. I want to share the kind of relationship that only stems from dreams. And that kind of relationship can only become a reality if two choose for it be. Does that kind of relationship intimidate you? If it does, I would advise that you run from me now. Because if you are what you project as being, your heart will be mine! But, don't get scared, it'd be safe cuz it'll be right next to mine...

Always,

$$\$\$\$\$\$$$

Dear...

I had to get at you ASAP so I could let you know just how much I enjoyed hearing your voice over the phone last night. I really had a great time!! To be honest, I have never felt as happy, as content or as excited hearing a voice as I was hearing yours. Though only for a few moments, I really enjoyed it.

Truthfully, (name), your whole vibe is top shelf! Even though we only met recently, I feel as though I've known you for a long time. I consider myself a pretty good judge of character, and from what you've shown me, you're a real woman. You seem unpredictable and exciting, yet so strong emotionally, and you also seem to have a loving and compassionate essence. You are so smart yet so humble and real. Last, but not least, you are so beautiful, yet not the least bit conceited.

All of these are traits that I look for in a woman.

(Name), whenever I think of you, my heart starts pounding, and my senses go into hyper mode when I think of you. You have become the Beyonce to my Jay, and I am drawn to you like a puppy to your favorite sandals.

Your loving friend,

$$$$$

Dearest...

How can I express the need I have to be with you? Words can't even express how I feel right now. It is as though I am on a GPS device and you're my destination. Constantly my thoughts are drawn to you, my love, you're constantly on my mind. (Name), my life so far away from you is empty and dull and my existence on this planet is too... like being in a black and white movie when my life could be in HD. I count the days until I can see you again.

Until that day is a reality, I remain.

Your true love,

$$$$$

What's up,

Just thought I'd write you a short note to tell you how much I enjoyed our phone call. I can't really remember when I had a more pleasurable time. Everything felt so natural and you were very easy to talk to. It's hard for me to identify what it is about you that attracts me so much. I guess it might be the combination of your sense of humor; your personality and your good looks. Whatever it is, I can sense its presence. You could call it chemistry, or better yet, the possibility that we're on the same wavelength.

(Name), I really hope that our first meeting wasn't our last because I felt very special when I was talking to you. Real talk: I want to give our friendship a chance to grow.

Well, I guess I've said enough for the time being. (Name), have a wonderful day, and hopefully, I'll see you real soon. If you get a chance, write me and tell me your thoughts. Until I hear from you again, take good care of yourself.

Always,

$$$$$

Dear Love,

I need you more than ever now... I need your love, I need love more than hope or money, wisdom or a drink...

Negativity kills the world around us and only your smile can turn the tide. When God said, "Let there be light," he gave us your face and body... and your hands are tender and your lips are sweet... and no one has eyes like yours.

You're right if you've thought the chance of our meeting was a miracle conceived in Heaven. It signaled the beginning of a true friendship which has provided me with a foundation on which to build a more meaningful life for myself. (Name), you'll never know how much that really means to me. I only hope and pray that our relationship will last for a long time and forever to come, for it provides me with a warmth I've never experience before.

Forever shall I hold you tender to my heart...

Love Always,

$$$$$

Babe,

Your fear of me not loving you as much as you want is nonsensical! Love, I love you! The longer I know you the more love I have. Even my jealousies are manifested from the extreme love I have for you. I would die for you! Yeah, I've stressed you out in the past, but every time I stress you out, it's about love. I can't help it. The last of your kisses are still on my lips; the last smile was the brightest; the last time I saw you walk away was the sexiest time I ever saw you walk. The last time I was with you I was filled with so much lust you'd think I just met you! I think you once said something about me only loving you cuz your looks. I can't believe you let that thought even cross your mind. My love revolves around your essence. Even if I was convinced that you didn't love me back

I would still be devoted to you. I have never felt this strong about anyone else in my whole life. Whenever I see you at visits my thoughts never stray, I'm completely captivated by you and your aura. The anxiety you're showing me right now is cool, but you don't need to worry about me not loving you for you, because I can promise you that I do. Trust me when I tell you that my whole world revolves around you.

Yours affectionately,

$$$$$

Dearest,

It is very important for me to express to you how much you really mean to me. I wish I could do this in person while holding you in my arms and staring into your eyes. But, since we are physically separated by these prison walls and miles of wasteland this expression must come in the form of letters such as this.

(Name), I know how hard it is for you as it is for me to be separated for so long. Life seems to be full of potholes that test our inner strength, and more importantly, our devotion and love for one another. After all, it is said that real love is limitless and overcomes all adversities. If this is real, it'll grow stronger every time something happens that tries to keep us apart.

(Name), our love has been assaulted many times, and I am convinced that it is love because the longer I am away from you the greater is my yearning to be with you again. You are my Queen and I am your devoted King. I cherish any thoughts of you, prize my memories of you which rises from the depths of my mind and live for the day when our physical separation will only be a memory.

Until that moment arrives, I send to you across the miles, all my love, all my hugs and my most passionate kiss.

Love always,

$$$$$

My Baby,

A moment does not pass without my thoughts turning to you, for my mind is linked directly to my heart where my passions are on fire. The truth is, your smile, quick–witted personality and intelligence attracts me so much that at times I can't stand the thought of even the shortest separation from you.

Just a short note to let my lovely Queen know that she is always with me in my heart. It is so difficult not being able to go home with you so that I can lie down between your thighs my love. Time has passed very slowly. Ever since we've been together— separated— you have been the focal point of all my thoughts. Fortunately, corresponding and visiting with you has given me something to live for so that loneliness I feel does not overwhelm me. Besides, it excites me to think that my letter will soon find its way into your warm loving hands and that your eyes will feast on my words. (Name), please don't delay your reply. I too need to feast. Until I hear from you once again, take very good care of what belongs to me. I love you very much and wait impatiently for the day that we are together forever...

Love,

$$$$$

Dear (Name),

When I think of the love and understanding that we share, I look to the sky and say, "Thanks to the Universe for giving me such a lovely woman." You are a major part of my life and I do cherish you. Due to my love for you, my main concern is your happiness. In whatever you do, I want you to be happy, but most of all, I want you to be happy with me. Your love inspires me, it drives me to hold my head up high knowing that I'm loved. I will always hold you dear to my heart regardless of the outcome of our future. All in all, I do have faith that we will be together no matter what situation arises.

There may be differences about us but we share the same love, the same thoughts and the same attraction towards each other. The love we share will always over–ride everything. Remember it is the significance of the love people share that holds them together.

You will always be respected and loved by me due to these simple facts: When I was lonely, you made me feel like I belonged, when I got sidetracked, you made me see things more clearly. You never gave up on me, even when I was ready to give up on myself. Everything is so much better for me now, because you saw something special in me and you helped me to realize the true meaning of love. How many people can say that they are truly loved? How many people feel sure deep down inside?

I am blessed to have you love me in all your convincing ways. I feel loved and I feel sure. And for all of that, I can only say "I will always try to give you many reasons to believe I truly love you too." Now, there is one thing I ask of you, and it's the same that I'll promise, and that's honesty. If we are to always grow together as we need and want to, we are to be honest with ourselves and each other, in the little things as well as the big things. This is what builds the trust that we really need to commit ourselves to one another. So let us promise honesty, even when it is not the easiest thing to give, because I believe that promise today will lead us to something very speical tomorrow.

I love sharing moments with you, because each conversation gives us a greater understanding of what we share. Who could ever forget a sunset whose colors seem to glow forever in our memories? Who could ever forget a rainbow whose grace moved us deep down inside?

Who could ever forget any wonderful thing, any beautiful thing that reminds us of just how precious our moments are together? Who could ever forget anything that makes us feel more alive or anything that makes us glad to be alive? I cannot forget them, and that is the reason why I can never forget you.

$$$$$

Love,

I sometimes think you really don't understand the depth of my love for you. You have put new meaning and awareness into my life. I know closeness when we are together, even though I appear distant at times. That's because of my surroundings.

I really care about you; it's important to me that you are safe, and important to me that you are well. I feel a sense of loss when we're apart; sometimes I wonder if we could not have more time together, then I think about the comfort of our nearness that keeps me going for a while. And, I know that we'll be together sooner than later.

Your touch will make all things right in my world. It always does. Wherever our decisions may take us, I will always care about you, I will always remember, there will always be a place for you in my heart.

$$$$$

Dear (Name),

I was just sitting here thinking 'bout life and I decided to share a lil' something with you. Baby, always listen to your own heart. You cannot listen to what others want you to do. You must listen to yourself. Society, family, friends and loved ones do not know what you must do. Only you know and only you can do what is right for you. So start right now. You will need to work very hard. You will need to overcome many obstacles. You will need to go against the better judgment of some people and you will need to bypass their prejudices. But you can have whatever you want if you try hard enough.

So start right now and you will live a life manifested by you and for you and you will love your life...

I want my Queen to be happy and learn to enjoy life. To understand that life can be great if you will only begin to see life for what it truly is and not to chase rainbows.

Please let me help you to become complete before life sweeps you away.

$$$$$

Baby,

Here is what I want for you. I want you to begin this day anew, with the thought of becoming the person you'll like to be. Today, I want you to set aside some time just for you...

To plan our future, to dream, to be honest with yourself about how you feel about us.

May you become better acquainted with the wonderful person you are.

Today I want my baby to experience something new. I want you to learn from the world around you; from the words you hear from me, the sounds you hear, the touches you feel and faces you see. Even through the course of your daily tasks, may you try to search for a new perspective, lean towards understanding and make the common place a wondrous place to be? Make your happiness... a happiness that lasts.

I want you to think of me and be warmed by knowing that I hold on to some very meaningful thoughts of you. May you have a gentle thanks for the sunrises and smiles along with the hardships and trials that have helped to get us to where we are today?

I wish you the kind of intuition that lets you know how naturally joy comes to those who open their eyes wide enough to envision it. I wish you the realization that by some interesting twist, doing for me is also doing for you.

I wish you the luxury of being reminded that having a sense of humor helps you to survive, and that even when everything else goes wrong, it pays such nice dividends to simply be glad you're a part of this moment in time! I wish you the simple pleasure of being alive.

May you listen to your inner needs and comply as best as you can. For today I wish you a little learning for your mind, as much love as your heart can hold, nourishment and exercise for your body and being able to see the beauty of the world... for your soul. Today I want you to think of the past only long enough to learn from it. And I hope you'll glance ahead into the future only for a fleeting dream you hope will come true. Today is your day. Your moment in time. Make it work... for you.

These are only some of my wishes for you today. Know that I love you and that I am with my girl.

$$$$$

Dear (Name),

I've finally finished (whatever you've been doing); now it's 1:00 a.m. and you're on my mind.

I was just thinking how fears, anxiety, tends to make people hesitate in allowing a relationship to grow. I mean, you have fears, I have fears, but we cannot allow them to impede us because as the world turns from day to day, as we live, we have to make decisions. Things sometimes don't turn out the way we want them to, but just because of that, should we live in a box and/or alienate ourselves from the world? Or, should we move on and make the best of things, because no matter what, things change. I just hope that as far as we're concerned, it is change for the better. Baby, we don't have a GPS to look into or know our future. I mean, you meet someone, you like them, you get to know them, you begin to love them, you make plans for so many things. Life has always been this way

26

so you must understand when I say there may be a storm ahead of us or sunshine; however, with you, even the storm is calm.

I am not infallible. If we were perfect we would be dead. So all that I can ask is that you have faith in me and know that I don't do anything on a whim. I'm not a push–button. I try to think everything through, dot all my I's and cross all my t's. You feeling me?

I guess what I'm trying to say is, whatever we have, we have. No one can take that away. You are my foundation, my salvation. In you, I see all my dreams becoming real. If this is love, then let it be. I don't know. All that I do know is you are the centerpiece of my thoughts. I once thought in singular, now it's plural. It amazes me how out of all the people in this world, God can make the path so that two will meet at just the right time in their lives. Isn't that amazing?

I will close here, Baby, so I can go to sleep and dream of you... Good night, my love.

$$\$\$\$\$\$$

Dear (Name),

Hello, my Queen, how is my sweetheart doing today? I pray that your every minute of the day be at peace. It will be soon to where I'll be taking the place of this letter which is being held in your hands. Honey, we are truly facing some hard times right now, but through it all, we will come out on top. I will continue to trust, love and respect you as my woman. Together we can overcome any obstacle. All it takes is a little willingness and effort. We must realize that anything that is worth having will never come with ease. We must understand this, because our relationship is worth having.

We have something that people spend millions of dollars trying to find; we share a special love and happiness with each other. I refuse to allow anything or anyone to come between what we have. I personally feel that is a once in a lifetime opportunity to share a love so special. My suggestion is, let's make the best of it because we only have one life to live. I'm willing to give my all to you if you're willing to do the same.

This is how we must visualize every bad situation, seeing where we can produce good out of bad situations. In God's perfect timing everything will fall in place, so let's not worry or stress about tomorrow, because tomorrow is already taken care of. Let's make the most of our relationship each day, and each day let's do everything in our power to do something beneficial for this relationship. I am always with you, through everyday activities and even when you lay at night to sleep, because I'm in your mind, your heart and your soul and you will never be without me.

$$$$$

Dear (Name),

Real talk, I just had an epiphany: I can be myself when I'm with you. My idea of romantic evenings include dim lights, soft music, and just the two of us. Because you make me feel like I have never felt before, I can tell you anything and you won't be shocked. Your undying faith is what keeps the flame of our love alive. You and me together, we can make magic. We're a perfect match. Thinking of you fills me with a wonderful feeling. Your love gives me the feeling that the best is still to come. You never give up on me and that's what keeps me going. You are simply irresistible. I love you because you bring the best out of me. You have a terrific sense of humor. Every time I look at you my heart misses a beat. You're the one who holds the key to my heart. You always say what I need to hear. You have taught me the true meaning of love. Love is what you mean to me... And you mean everything! You are my theme for a dream. I have had the time of my life and I owe it all to you. And, of course, you're intelligent cause you were smart enough to fall in love with me! Smile!

Love always,

$$$$$

Man, what's up, love!?

I'm having a great day today and you know why that is? It's because of you!!! You are my reassurance that something is good in my life. Has it occurred to you that I really love you? Not just the words but how I really feel about you? In spite of our ups and downs I do care and love you very much. You are my best friend and no one can ever take that away because you were here at a time when I needed a friend so desperately.

Thank you for the day we met. Ever since the day we connected, I knew that you were extremely special. I knew that I wanted to make you my baby and I knew then that my emotions had been touched. Ever since the connection I knew we would be bonded forever. I knew that I wanted to share everything about myself with you.

I knew even then that I would grow as a person. Ever since then I knew that we had a very poignant relationship. I knew that by body and mind we would be passionate forever. If we had not connected I would still be searching for my baby and I would still be thinking that love was not real. So, I sincerely thank you for the day we met.

I love my Queen. You've been a very powerful instrument these past (how long). Saying the words thank you does not necessarily give the strength behind how I really want to express myself. THANK YOU!

I love you.

$$$$$

Ma,

I know that it disturbs you that I don't write you as often as I should, but you must know by now how difficult is for me to compose a letter. For some people it's easy, but I have the hardest time expressing myself. Even though my feelings for you are strong, at times I cannot, for the life of me, find the proper words to describe them. It really is frustrating because I love you very much. Love, you're the only woman in my life and I need you to realize this.

(Name), being so far away from your loving arms is pure torture. It's as if you're a powerful transmitter and I am a receiver. You are on all of my frequencies. Nothing else can get through, and my days are spent endlessly under you universal influence. (Name), I can't believe all these words are coming to me as easily as they are. Could it be that I'm finally getting the hang of it, or is it that you inspire me so? I think it's the latter. How can I help but not be inspired by your all–encompassing beauty and charm?

My love, I want you to know that I can hardly wait for the day when I return home to your waiting arms. That truly will be one of the happiest moments of my life.

Until that day is a reality, I remain.

Your eternal love,

$$$$$

My dearest...

I just gotta let you know something: I wake up every morning thinking of you. Your photos and our intoxicating (visits/phone calls) which we spend on the weekends have my senses in turmoil. Sweet, incomparable (Name), what a strange effect you have on my heart. Are you my moon? Do I give you enough light to reflect? Is my baby okay being out there all by herself? You have no idea how my soul aches with sorrow, and there can be no rest for your lover; but is there still more in store for me when, holding onto these feelings, I draw from your lips, from your heart, a love which consumes me with fire?

I'll be (seeing/talking to) my love soon. My little girl. My baby.

Until then, ma douce mon amour, a thousand kisses; but give me none in return, for they set my blood on fire.

Love,

$$$$$

Love,
 I just woke up filled with thoughts of you. Your photo and the intoxicating visit which we spent (yesterday/today) have left my senses in a turmoil. Sweet, incomparable (Name), what a strange effect you have on my heart! Are you angry? Do I see you looking sad? Are you worried? My soul aches with sorrow, and there can be no rest for your lover; but is there still more in store for me when I draw from your lips, from your heart, a love which consumes me with fire? Ah! It was our last (visit/ phone conversation) that I fully realized how false an image of you your photo gives!!

Love always,

$$$$$

Dear (Name),
 For the sake of loving communication there is something I want you to know about me and about my feelings... It's that I don't think I've ever been so happy... or so afraid in all my life. I'm scared because of what I've gone through before with love; I feel like it's taken me a long time to pick up the pieces of my life and put them back together again.
 Just when I started feeling comfortable with life, in a lonely sort of way, you came along... and now I know that there is nothing I'd rather do than love... and be loved... by you.
 Just don't ever go away, okay? The only things I want to leave are my feelings of being afraid. You do understand (name), don't you baby? I want everything about you and our tomorrows together to stay.

Your lover,

$$$$$

31

Boo!

There are things in life which are inevitable; I am powerless to control them. The sun will rise and set, the tide will come in and go out, the seasons will change, the birds will fly south for the winter and return in the spring and the caterpillar will transform itself into a beautiful butterfly.

Babe, I believe that our love is blessed by God. It is a union of two spirits destined for everlasting happiness. You have become the star of my life which brings me light in this dark world and warmth when I need it. You offer me promise of renewal, the joy of living, the peace of mind which comes from sharing and caring and that shoulder to lean on in times of stress. You are my swallow from Capistrand, my precious butterfly, and I will cherish you and love you forever!

Love,

$$$$$

My dear (Name),

I already miss you and your car is probably still on the freeway half–way home.

How can you ask me if I truly love you? Can you not feel me inside of you every awakening moment? Before closing your eyes at bedtime, do I come to mind? How about you're wakening moments the very next morning. Do I come to your thoughts? If your answer is yes... well, you've answered your own question.

For that kind of intense feeling isn't easily administered. It took time, patience, understanding, giving and taking.

But to make a long story short, yes, I do love you. Yes, you are my soulmate, and yes, I will protect you and take care of you from this day forward.

I love you...

$$$$$

32

Hello My Moon,

I'm sorry that it has taken me so long to write, there is no reason that I could give for my delay that is worthy of your acceptance. I have been diligently trying to catch up on my legal work. I have been so engrossed in it that I have excluded all else. Now that I am caught up the next thing on my agenda is you.

You can't imagine how much I miss you; I can still smell and feel you. I know now that you must come to me because now the illusion has become real. For (whatever) years you were just a dream to me gracing my nights and mesmerizing my days, a being I created in my fantasies. However, on (date) you became flesh and I will never let you go. God sent me you and to not take care of this gift is an insult to Him and I would never commit such sacrilege. Damn it, you should feel guilty for making me miss you like this!

Baby, you have come inside my purgatory and offered yourself as my salvation and for this I thank you and I will forever be in your debt, so hurry and come to me so that my payments may begin.

Love,

$$$$$

Dear (Name),

I am sitting here in a depressed mood reflecting back on my life and I have come to the conclusion that had you been in my life earlier I wouldn't be here now.

You are the only person who understands me, the only person who doesn't think I'm just a dreamer. Only you can see my vision, everyone else thinks because I'm incarcerated I could never do these things that I want to do, but you actually think that I can!

It's the fact that you really believe in me that makes you so special to me. Only you have it and since this is the case you will be the only one who will help me enjoy it.

33

You say that I'm not affectionate. Well, in a sense, you're right. Under these circumstances I find it hard to be, but I will try harder and I do think you will see a big difference in me once I'm out.

I have placed the most important part of me in your hands where I feel it is safe. You have my trust and there is nothing more important than that.

People search all of their lives in hope of finding their individual utopias, that idyllic existence that's filled with happiness and love; however, sometimes in their attempt to find this place they fail to see that they already have it. You know, there is an ancient Babylonian saying that says, "the name of God is mother on the lips and in the hearts of children" and the reason for this is (I think), children feel an unconditional love so intense that it must be inspired by God.

Love is the emotion that makes one look forward to being alive, it makes you smile, and feels so good inside, it creates a trust so strong that deceit is unthinkable. It creates a haven so secure that harm is inconceivable.

I want you to feel good inside, I want to make you smile and feel alive, I want to create a trust so strong that deceit is unthinkable and a haven so secure that harm inconceivable. Do I love you?

I do love you…

$$$$$

Baby,

Once again, I send you a letter with hope that it finds you well and in good spirits.

In all honesty, whenever you are gone, the emptiness of my situation becomes unbearable, and I turn to corresponding with you as a pastime which helps dampen the loneliness of the moment.

(Name), my love for you can only be measured in a mathematical form, and that in itself falls far short of its true magnitude. For you are the nourishment of my spirit; consequently, you are my strength. When we are together, you provide that electric potential which gives my life that spark of vitality. When we are apart such as now, I get butterflies in my stomach as if in anticipation of our reuniting, that "Opening Night" which is sure to come. (Name), each time (I look in your eyes/hear your voice), I'm drawn into the farthest reaches of your mind's inner world. There I find a land of compassion, of understanding and of love and, by some good fortune, I also find myself as one of its inhabitants. For this I am very grateful.

Until we are together again in each other's embrace, I remain, Your eternal love.

$$$$$

(Name),

How can I properly express the joy I derived from reading your last letter? I must tell you that it lifted my spirits to heights undreamed, a very welcome change from where and I pray that you will not stop writing them.

My love, I want you to know that I am well, and that my situation here is okay. In all honesty though, it could never compete with home, for boredom and loneliness are my constant companions. But enough of this kind of talk for now! I hope you are well and in good spirits because if you are not I could never hope to be. Right now, I truly wish I could hold you in my arms and kiss your soft supple lips. What a heavenly thought, if only but daydream.

(Name), you mean the world to me! I can't imagine life without you. How empty it would be! In truth, only a love poem of classic dimension could express my love for you. Although I am not a poet, I have always wanted to write you such a poem. Unfortunately, in the past, I lacked the discipline to attempt it. Lately though, I've had a lot of time on my hands and in my own inadequate way, I finally gave it a try. I think

35

you'll find the thought is there even though the poem may be lacking in technique. So, here it is! I hope you like it.

(Insert Poem Here)

Love, I can't think of anything more to add at this time. So, until I hear from you, I wish you the best of health and send my deep and everlasting love.

$$$$$

To the love of my life:

Did you know... That there is no one in my world besides you with whom I can spend an entire day doing whatever comes along with never a thought for anyone else, feeling completely satisfied because we are together?

Did you know... That here is no one besides you whom I can talk to openly and honestly, knowing our love will only grow and feeling a need for nothing but conversation?

Did you know... That there is no one more comfortable for me than you— whom I can enjoy silence with and never have a need to fill the space between us because there is no space?

$$$$$

Dear (Name),

Thank you for the wonderful visit. Today I truly observed your love for me. Today you revealed how much you are willing to give to me. How much you are willing to listen and not just feel. Today I feel truly blessed.

I can feel you coming into me, giving yourself without the feared fight. Here again I'm beginning to feel whole again now that you have truly returned to me. Different? Yes, you are very much different. I've strived very hard to get you to where you are today.

Later... At last, it's time to get to bed. How's my girl?

How am I feeling? At this point it's difficult to describe. Maybe I could, I'm just content with the thought of your coming home to me. I can't say that I'm elated or anything like that, simply because it feels so natural that you should be here. It would be different if I had just met you and you landed in my lap. That would be a blessing from the Gods. But I've found you! I mean I have really put in lots of work to get you into my heart, so therefore I'm feeling that you just naturally belong to me.

I do feel better knowing that all my work was not in vain. Never before have I put so much into something that I really wanted and didn't receive. You have been the first and that really was starting to make me feel some type of way. I guess you can call it fear, but I know better than to let negative thoughts fester in my mental. Living in fear takes away from life's pleasures. (Name), there is so much more that I feel like I can teach you. I can sense that this is the right time because you seem to be more open to my wisdom these days. If you just continue to listen to me, I promise you everything will turn out okay... better than okay—LOVELY! Till the next time, I love you,

$$$$$

Love,
We gotta talk. There's a recurring thought on my mind and its how much you need to be reassured that I love you. I love you. And I truly understand, especially after you made me to understand our circumstances. Now, I'll be more conscious in that area. Our relationship has shifted into another realm so I gotta catch up. But instead of being in a situation where I have to constantly remind you that my affection for you is real, I'd rather just show you by my actions.

(Name), I love you. There is no lie when I say how you turn me on. I enjoy your company immensely. Teaching you new thoughts and ideas is my pleasure. Even now I can see how you're growing. And I think you and I are heading in a direction towards oneness and completion.

You told me that it's getting harder for you to write me letters. That they sound boring to you. That's crazy! You can sit there and write me anything and I would love to read it because it's coming from your mental. I want you to share your true feelings with me. Feelings of love can never sound boring. Stop trying to censor yourself.

You owe it to yourself to go all the way this one time before leaving this earth. To fight against yourself would be to refuse what God made ready for you.

(Name), I promise you that you have never been taught love or reasoning. What a tragic and serous dilemma First of all, why would I leave something that I've put my all into? Why would I desert something that has been my biggest help, and furthermore, can help me shine harder than I ever have in my whole life?

I love you,

$$$$$

Greetings from (name of city)! I hope this letter finds you well. Since I last (spoke/ heard/saw) you, I've been very busy with my researching my case. I've wanted to write you for a minute now, but it seems like every time I get started something comes up and I have to stop. I hope you can understand how that is.

(Name), I often think of that wonderful evening when we (first met/the first time I saw you/the first time we spoke to each other/the first time we touched/the first time we kissed). It seems just like yesterday because I keep such precious memories constantly alive in the pages of my mind.

(Name), I just haven't been the same since I met you. Knowing that you are in this world excites me and makes my body tingle all over. I get butterflies in my stomach, and my heart skips a beat.

Please write me and let me know how you're doing, even if it's just a short note. Until I hear from you, or better yet, until we meet again, my thoughts are with you.
Your loving friend,

$$\$\$\$\$\$$

My Better Half,

I kinda feel a lil' stupid. I mean, I talk to you on the phone every day and here I am writing. I guess the only reason why I'm doing it is because I'm just used to thinking about you. What am I gonna do about this? I'm starting to get a lil' nervous about having you as such a large part of my thoughts.

But, for real though, I do have a reason for writing you right now. I promised myself that I'll do whatever is needed to keep you happy today, tomorrow and the tomorrows after that. If it ever comes to a point where I'm slipping in my responsibilities, all you have to do is point the problem out to me and it will be fixed. That, I promise!

Each day, each hour, each minute that we're apart is an eternity. Thoughts of you flood my mind with desire, and at times, I can't bear our separation. Love, it's as if a part of me is missing and that is very distressing.

I know that in time we'll be together forever and a day. And this knowledge consoles me to a degree. However, it can't take away the pain and anguish of the moment. Only your presence can do that.
Always...

$$\$\$\$\$\$$

Dear (Name),

I'm just lying here thinking how lucky I am to have

someone like you in my life.

Thinking of you seems to lower my blood pressure, put me at ease. Knowing that you're in my corner makes me realize that I'm the luckiest man on earth. I wish so badly that I could show you how much I appreciate you. It makes me so upset knowing that I'm not able to prove to you in every way that I'm serious about our relationship. All my life I've been searching for that special love; the kind of love that'll be there through thick and thin; a love to call my own, an unconditional love.

I really feel like you were meant to be in my life, and it's a trip 'cuz you came into my life at a time when I really needed you, and I gotta tell you, you've been there since you got here.

I'm patiently waiting for the day when I'll be able to make you see how much I really do want to be with you, because I just want to take away all your doubts. (Name), I'm not asking for much, I just want you to love me and be here for me through these dark times of my life. There is nothing more important to me than having you in my life sweetheart. I need your love and support and I promise you, you won't regret having me in your life, because I'm going to love you like you've never been loved before. I'm going to give you an everlasting love that will stand the test of time. You mean the world to me and I'll be destroyed if you ever left me. Honestly, I don't think I can handle even the thought of losing you.

Right now, all I can give you is my word. I'm limited in my actions now, but the day will come when I will be a free man and then and only then can I show you how much you really mean to me. I know that you've taken a long time and you won't regret the chance that you've taken with me.

In ending this letter, let me say thank you for the card, thank you for the letters, thank you for the money, thank you for your time, but most of all, thank you for you!!!

$$$$$

Dear (Name),

It is always a pleasure receiving mail form you, thank you so much.

Well, it brings joy to me to know that things are working out a little better on your behalf; you deserve it.

Yeah, I plan on coming and being with you when I get out. I miss hearing your beautiful voice on the phone; your voice truly eases my mind. Anyway, I'm taking this situation one day at a time and being strong in the process. Of course, having you in my corner helps a lot.

(Name), I can't wait to hold you in my arms real tight and kiss you for a very long time. I remember when you came to see me at (wherever) and I kissed you when you were leaving; your kiss was sweet to my mouth. The only reason I didn't kiss you longer is because the guards don't like it. I remember sitting at the table talking to you and looking into your eyes. I could see the love and concern you have for me. (Name),   I can't wait until I'm released this summer. We're gonna rule the world! Please just hold on a little bit longer. It'll be over before you know it. We've come a long way together and when I think back to how and when we first met, I have to say we were meant to be together, because if not, I'm sure we wouldn't have met.

$$\$\$\$\$\$$$

To the moon in my solar system, why do I love you so much? You're under the impression that I gave you my love too easily and that it means it's not real. It's like since you've been hurt before, you don't want to trust anyone who shows you the slightest bit of affection. And, real talk, if I were you I'd probably feel the same way too. But then again, what if you were in my shoes? How would you feel if I didn't believe that you loved me? How would you feel?

How many women can measure up to you? You love me. I mean you "really" love me. And you would do anything for the betterment of our relationship. I know it even if you don't say it. I love you because you made me aware of who I am. I love you because you force me to think. I love you because you make my future look bright. I love you because I can trust and depend on you. I love you because you are sensual, passionate, soft and as understanding as you can be within you. I love the woman that you are. I love the bitch that you can be. I love your soft hands and your sweet lips. I love your luscious breast and the phat ass that I'll one day get to dig up in. I love the adventure that lies beneath the surface in which I will use to bring our dreams into reality.

I love your heart, though it appears to be weak at this point. I love the way that you love me. I love you because you love me enough to throw everything else away that you once believed in. I love you for the way you make me feel. I love you for the inspiration in which you give me. Oh, damn, baby, I love you for sooo many reasons in which you cannot begin to understand until later. I could go on and on but I won't. I won't only because I'm too stirred up to continue. I stirred up cuz I'm in love!

I love you!

$$\$\$\$\$\$$

Dear...

I pray that this letter finds you healthy and in good spirits because your well being has always been my foremost concern. My love, I am as well as can be expected, even though at this point in time my life is far from ideal. Our separation has cast a cloud of loneliness and stress over me, and I know I won't be right till the next time I see you.

(Name), there are many things I desire to tell you and I

have many passions yearning for expression. Yet it seems as though I'm always at a loss of words. This flaw of mine gets on my last nerve!

Yesterday I was reading a book of poetry to help me subdue my loneliness when I came across a love poem which, to my amazement, expresses to perfection all of my inner thoughts, desires and feelings. Truthfully, I couldn't believe my eyes for it was written many years ago by (Name of Poet).

Love, as you read it, try to think not of the poet, but of me, for its verses express the sentiments of my heart.
(Insert Poem)

With eternal love and devotion, I send you my most passionate kiss and remain,
Yours forever,

$$$$$

Babe,

Can you tell that you are making me happy? Can you? If you were to just feel for one minute, just let your inner soul simply feel, you can feel my energy flowing through your veins. We are one.

When we touch, you will feel my soul throughout your body. Your insides will tremble and perhaps your outer layer also. But most importantly, you will know from that day on who you belong to.

Now please hear my words on this matter. (Name), I don't want you to be afraid anymore. Let your mind be at ease... I might as well request that you stop thinking about me for that matter. The only thing that will stop you from tripping is when I hold you in my arms. That will put all to rest...
Love you Ma.

$$$$$

(Name),

Why are we wasting time? Just admit it, you're mine, you're too wonderful not to be. I appreciate you like you've never been appreciated before.

This obstacle, even though it's tiny, so tiny I already forgot his name, is insignificant to me because I know that a flower can't blossom on desolate ground. You are the only beautiful thing in this desert that I'm living in. You need to come on home.

Don't fight it, love. I want you; don't ask me why because I don't question my instincts. I just follow them and they'll tell me that you have a significant role in my future and I won't deny it. I will sample the pleasures of your body. I will bask in the revelations of your mind and the most important thing that I will do is love you.

Come home, baby. This'll be the only way for you to truly experience happiness. Let me shatter this illusion that you're living in so we can start anew.

It's our destiny,

$$$$$

Dear (Name),

It's late and I can't sleep. My mind is wondering about many things. It's not considered as worrying, but just speculations. As always, I desire to know what your feelings are. In order for this relationship to be secured, we must be individually secure within ourselves. There should be no doubts between us. There should be no dishonesty. There should be no misleading at any time for any reason.

My point is, what we have is beautiful and we should never do anything to discourage this bond we've created. I know that no one's perfect and just like any other man, I definitely have my set of faults. I'm human, so I'm prone to lie, cheat, love, hurt and what have you, but I must say, knowing you has made me near perfect, or at least as close as I've ever been.

If I were to compare myself to any tangible object, my choice would be a mirror, because I tend to reflect whatever I see. There's an old saying that says, "You looked with love and love returns."

$$$$$

(Name, Name, Name),

Your name is pure music to my ears. For real, I could call it out loud a million times and never tire of its sound.

(Name), believe me when I say not a second goes by without my thoughts turning to you. At this very moment, I wish you were here so I could hold you and kiss you. I couldn't get tired of that either.

You gotta know that it's getting harder for me to play the role that I'm not trippin' off this time without you. It's like I'm falling into a depression. All the homies tell me to snap out of it and get back to the usual me, but I can't. I can't stop thinking about you and missing you. How can I snap out of this when I'm so far away from you?

Yesterday, I saw someone on TV who looked like you and I had to look twice. You know, something deep down in my heart was hoping against all hope that, by some miracle, it was really you on TV and not some stranger. Truthfully, this has been happening to me a lot lately, and each time my disappointment increases. Sometimes I wonder just how I'm going to last another (weeks/months) before seeing you again.

(Name), the fact is if it weren't for your letters and phone conversations, my loneliness would be killing me. They really keep me going and are a source of great relief. Real talk, I crave them with a passion and whenever one arrives at mail call, my heart races with anticipation, for the words which lie within are my only direct bridge to you.

Your Eternal Love,

$$$$$

Love,

Just a quick thought that I wanna share with you. It is so very rare to find someone in a lifetime that you can become close to and friends with. It takes a special bond to bring two people together, a lot of patience and understanding. A sprinkle of mischief for the good times, and an abundance of laughter. If you're lucky, you find someone you can love, someone who is what you have been to me lately, my best friend.

I love you...

$$$$$

Hey Babe,

Of course it's one thing to write little words of love on a greeting card. However, an entirely different matter to sit down and dig deep within the walls of one's being. Coming from this place in one's soul isn't a very easy task to say the least.

You know as well as I that I have been putting you off as if to say "We'll tend to your needs later." I'm guilty of this crime without a word of denial.

Why?

It's kinda simple. You and you alone are my only salvation. That scares the fuck outta me. I'm in constant fear that at any given moment you will flee from me and leave me exposed to allowing some space of void to enter into my life. That is why I sometimes want to let you go, but only when I seem to have built up some form of self–protection. Actually, I know deep within that this self–protection can easily be blown away. Yet it frightens me more to be caught off guard when my very life is more exposed to the pain of losing someone that means so very much to me. I am thoroughly tired of losing the very few that are dear to my heart.

No, I don't expect that you nor anyone else will ever understand the true essence of my being. It always comes across as if I'm beating my own drum. From yours and others point of view, I'm full of myself. Which is hardly the truth, and yet there is no way I can defend myself without coming across like I'm conceited. Somewhat like an attorney defending himself in a criminal trial. He must use "I" "I" "I" "I" throughout the trial. And I know that gets real boring real quick.

You have no idea how scared I am about how you might react to my behavior once I'm released. Hell, I don't even know how I will react to my returned freedom. All I do know is that my largest fear is your fleeing from me for lack of understanding of something that is most definitely bigger than both of us.

In order for me to tell you that there is something inside of me that is compelling me towards something magnificent, it loses its strength in the translation.

What I do know is that you need to play a major role in this event. This I know cuz I can feel deep in my soul.

You want me to be ordinary and yet my ordinariness is the thing that attracts you to me most of all. Life truly is a paradox.
I love you,

$$$$$

Angel,
Have I ever sent you any greeting cards? No. Today

47

someone was transferred and I noticed that he left a lot of junk behind. But something told me to reach down and read what was in the envelope and I found these words. I really don't believe in greeting cards because I feel that more words have more strength. But will you explain the words, or shall I say the message on the card really is how I truly feel? I never thought that something you can buy for two dollars could hold such a deep message. So from now on I give you my word that I will periodically search for deep meanings in even the smallest things because I just learned from experience that you can never know where something special will come from.
Love Always,

$$$$

(Name),

I'm sure that for some time now you've been wondering how deep is my love for you. Even though I would love to hold you in my arms and stare into your eyes as I tell you the following words I have to come to you this way because of my situation.

I love you this much...

Enough to do anything for you...

Give my life, love, my heart, and my soul to you and for you. Enough to willingly give all of my time, efforts, thoughts, talents, trust and prayers to you. Enough to want to protect you, care for you, guide you, hold you, comfort you, listen to you and cry to you and with you. Enough to be completely comfortable with you, act silly around you, never have to hide anything from you and be myself with you...

I love you enough to share all of my sentiments, dreams, goals, fears and worries, my entire life with you. ENOUGH to want the best for you, to wish for your successes, and to hope for the fulfillment of all your endeavors. ENOUGH to keep my promises to you and pledge my loyalty and faithfulness to you. ENOUGH to cherish your friendship, adore your personality, respect your values and see you for who you are.

I love you enough to fight for you, compromise for you, and sacrifice myself for you if need be. ENOUGH to miss you incredibly when we're apart, no matter what length of time it's for and regardless of the distance. ENOUGH to believe in our relationship, to stand by it through the worst of times, to have faith in and strength as a couple and to never give up on us. ENOUGH to spend the rest of my life with you, be there for you when you need or want me, and never, never, ever want to leave you or live without you.

So you see (Name), I love you this much and then some.

Forever yours,

$$$$$

Love,

Just as a poet needs inspiration to write a masterpiece, I need you...
Just as an artist needs a subject for his work of art, I need you...
Just as a teacher needs a pupil to mold into greatness, I need you...
Just as a composer needs a theme to create a timeless melody, I need you...

For without you, (Name), my life will be empty of all inspiration. There will be no works of art for me to stare at; no person of greatness before me; no timeless melody to listen to. My life will exist in shades of gray instead of vibrant colors and I will be less than whole.

In the past, the proper words have escaped me and my innermost feelings have been kept locked away in the depths of my heart. No more, for through this letter, I proclaim to you (Name), my undying love and eternal devotion.

Yours forever,

$$$$$

Dear (Name),
A lil while ago when we were on the phone you asked me what I thought it would be like when we finally get to meet. I've thought about this deeply in order to give you an honest answer: I see you in the visiting room. I see us. I see you sitting there nervous, wondering how will you greet me and I you. You're thinking; "What the hell am I doing in a place like this?" You're wondering what kind of power I have to have pulled you to me. These are the thoughts running through your mind.
As I enter the visiting room you'll stand with uncertainty to approach me. I smile and give you a kiss from across the room. Your smile becomes a bigger smile. I walk toward you and open my arms for an embrace. You wrap your arms around me and hold me for a while not wanting to let go. Probably because you don't know what to expect after that. So, I brake the embrace and say "Give me a kiss, Ma." As our lips touch I can sense a warm sensation surging throughout your body.
During the visit I will tease you a lot. We will laugh. I will see your guard melt before my eyes. We will talk. Talk about many things. Plans will unfold before your mind's eye. Your heart will thump heavily inside your chest. You will feel the awesome impact of love.
Hurry to me...

$$$$$

Babe,
Each day, each hour, each minute we are apart is an

eternity. Thoughts of you flood my mind with desire, and, at times I can't bear our separation. My love, it feels as if a part of me is missing and that is very distressing.

I know that, in time, we will be together again and this knowledge consoles me to a small degree. However, it can never take away the pain and anguish of the moment. Only your presence can do that.

(Name), you are the light of my life, the nourishment of my soul, the essence of my being and your love gives me the strength to carry on until that wonderful day when we are reunited, I remain totally in your thoughts and spirit.

Love always,

$$$$$

Good morning, love...

Our arms are empty of each other for a moment only. How beautiful you turn... Your mouth tilts to let my kisses in. Lie still... We shall be longer.

We need so little room, we two... thus on a single pillow, as we move nearer, nearer heaven until I burst inside you like a screaming rocket.

Then we are quietly apart... returning to this earth.

Your friendship provides me with more than just companionship; it gives to me a sense of belonging like I've never felt before. It lights my path through the darkness which surrounds me and gives me hope for a brighter future. Such a friendship instills within me a warmth which overcomes the biting chill of an impersonal world and kindles the fire of love.

Even though I have much more to say, I guess I should conclude this note. It's getting quite late and tomorrow provides me a great day because I shall be visiting with you.

Tonight, as I lie in bed, I will be thinking of you, and as I drift off to sleep, your pretty smile will be the last wonderful image of the day. My dear (Name), until the next time, I send

to you all the love I possess along with ten thousand times ten thousand kisses.
Love,

$$$$$

Dear (Name),

I know it's been quite some time since I last wrote. Believe me, it's not because I didn't think of you these past (2/3/4) weeks/days, but because I could not find the proper words to express my true feelings for you.

(Name), I realize that a long–distance romance can be quite difficult to maintain, but I know in my heart that you are well worth the effort. To me, you're a very special person, and I'm deeply and undeniably attracted to you.

(Name), you're the most attractive woman I have ever known. Every time we are together, your eyes melt me into submission and your gentle caress makes my body tremble with excitement. Your alluring smile and cheerful, loving nature always lifts my spirits and brings joy into my darkened life.

Hopefully, if all goes well, you'll be able to come up and see me soon. To be honest, I can hardly wait to be with you again. I hope you feel the same. For now, take care of yourself and write me. I promise to reply faster the next time.

With deep and sincere affection, I remain,
Your loving friend,

$$$$$

Love,

For me, (Valentine's Day/Christmas/Thanksgiving) this year will be a day of loneliness and despair. How can it be otherwise with you on the other side of the fence? While other lovers are embracing I will be sitting here alone thinking of you. How unfair it is for us to be apart on such a (special day/romantic day). (Name), were it in my power, I would conjure up some special spell and transport you into my cell. Unfortunately, that is just another dream and somehow I must resolve myself to the reality of our situation. So, in lieu of a warm embrace, I send you through this note, my deepest and most sincere (whatever day) love.

I love you...

$$$$$

Dear...

How are you? I hope this letter finds you healthy and in good spirits. Everything has been going smoothly for me and I've been keeping quite busy with (law research, whatever).

(Name), the last time I was with you I enjoyed myself more than you can ever imagine. I really felt great with you by my side because I'm attracted to you far more than I have ever been to any other woman. It's as though we are the two remaining pieces of a puzzle, which when joined together complete the whole picture.

To tell you the truth, I've been thinking about you constantly, your beautiful face smiling at me and your delightfully curvaceous body standing near me. I hear your sexy voice calling my name and feel your warm embrace. As I relive these times, my body trembles with anticipation and I get butterflies in my stomach.

(Name), dreaming of the past with you is not enough to satisfy my passions. I need to be with you again. I need to experience those special feelings which I get only when I am at your side. So please write me quick and tell me when I can expect our next visit. Until I hear from you, take very good care of yourself.

Love,

$$$$$

(Name), Love...

Why are you trippin'? Come on, Love! Don't you understand that life is too short for us to be on this off brand shit? (Name), I've learned to love you so much and I can't see myself with anyone else. So, tell me, where are you getting this nonsense from?

What good are you there when your heart is with me? Now is the time to show and prove. You need to jump out there and show the world that you're willing to go all in with me.

Please, Love, don't do this to us. I need you. You need me. You are my best friend, my lover, the only friend and lover I'll ever want. You're smart, you're sexy. There's so much to us that I know we can't be beat!

Love, please hear my pleas. Why torture the one person that loves you the most? I need you. I want you. Please come home. Please come on home...

$$$$$

Dear (Name),

You know, (Name), Kurkegaard says that "instinct is the most intelligent of intelligence." My instincts scream when I think of you. Therefore, I think I should investigate this thing that has awakened this dormant phenomenon of mine. I was told that you are intelligent, charming, loyal and attractive, these are qualities that are precious, "very precious" and I would love to be the recipient of them, so let me formally introduce myself.

My name is (name), pleased to meet you. I am originally from (where), my interests are you! Because the thought of you fascinates me!

Sweetheart, I am a cards on the table kind of guy that will never lie to you. Don't get me wrong, I am not pious by any stretch of the imagination. It's just that I feel lying is a weakness; therefore a liar is weak. The magnificent qualities that you possess should be kept in a citadel of strength and I would love to be this citadel for you.

I would never abuse you, because what would I gain by abusing the one thing that will probably become the closest thing to me?

I know this introduction letter is somewhat forward. Forgive me, it's just that I don't beat around the proverbial bush. You already know that you are wonderful so there is no need for frivolous blandishments that don't really mean anything. A relationship, whether platonic or something more meaningful, is only as strong as it's foundation, and there is no stronger foundation than one built of honesty and mutual understanding, so be warned that I intend to learn everything about you and my need for this knowledge is for the sole purpose at enhancing my ability to please you, so write soon so that my lessons may begin.

$$\$\$\$\$\$$

(Name),

It's a pleasure having you as a friend. You never cease to prove your love for me, you are that rainbow that displays its eloquence in the midst of the rain in my life. You are that bridge over troubled waters. Your love is like the sun above which shines in my life. I cherish your love, I respect you as a woman, a true woman. You are truly a blessing in my life sent from God! You are that angel which holds my hand and walks with me through the storm.

I will always remember your kindness and cherish everything that you do to elevate this relationship we share.

Please continue to be strong for me, it's just a matter of time before we embrace each other. It is our destiny that we are together, so please don't allow time to come between us, because time is only destiny in motion. I'll be with you soon. Love,

$$$$$

Dear (Name),
We've come so far together through these difficult times. You've truly shown me the true meaning of love and understanding. I never thought we would become so deep into each other and now that we've come this far, there's no time to go backward. I definitely don't have time for games or time to waste. I've wasted enough time out of my life from being in here. When I'm released from this place, there will be nothing that will stop me from getting to where you are. (Name), I don't want to be anything but real with you, we should have no secrets from each other, we must be honest at all times no matter what the situation may be. We can have a beautiful friendship, relationship and love life.

I don't have long to go in this place, all you have to do is stay strong and do what you have to do. Continue to show your love in my direction, continue to be true and honest. We have many things to see and do together when I'm released. There is nothing we can't accomplish if we put our minds to it. Baby, please stay focused. I know that you are a strong woman and I need your support through these difficult times. Everything will pay off in the end. Just be patient and you'll see.

I send my love to you across the friendly blue sky; you're forever in my thoughts and in my heart.

$$$$$

(Name),

What we have for each other is love. No one ever said that love was easy. Sometimes love can hurt. It can be disappointing at times also. Sometimes love can cause tears as well as fears, but one thing I've learned about love is once you are truly in it, you can never really get out of it. Mentally you may be able to tell yourself that you are not in love with that someone anymore, but within your heart, the love is crying out.

Love has two sides, a down side and an upside, and I've basically mentioned some of the down side's emotions of love, but, it also can bring joy. Love can make you feel confident, it can make you feel meaningful, wanted, special, accepted and overwhelmingly happy.

It can give you a peace of mind, it can make you smile and it can make your eyes sparkle like the midnight stars. The thing that makes love so special is taking the bitter with the sweet, because by doing this, it creates a love that is unbreakable.

Love reminds me of unique drink called lemonade. For example, if you take a bitter lemon and mix it with sugar and water you create a drink with such a unique taste. In order for us to taste that unique flavor of love we must be able to accept the bitter with the sweet.

Sweetheart, I know without a doubt that we will make it through this, so stay focused, stay strong and please stay my lady.

$$$$$

Love,

Your happiness is my main concern. I know and understand that you are faced with the pressures of the world every day, and in order to overcome these pressures, it is required for you to put a lot of time into your everyday schedule. It is good to know that I am in your thoughts every day because you are definitely in mine.

As I think of how fast this year has gone by, I realize that real soon I'll be on the streets once again and I'll be with you to help you and encourage you with your plans as well as mine. I truly look forward to seeing you, kissing, touching and spending time with you. This past year has brought us closer to each other. We've faced many trials and tribulations, but we've overcome them all and we must continue to do so. Keep faith in us, keep focused, and most of all, keep love.

CHAPTER THREE

MASTER AT COMMUNICATION (MAC)

Everything I say or do is calculated right down to the last syllable. It has to be. Since I'm a Mathematician/Scientist, I'm in the know about the fact that every action has a reaction. This means I think before I speak, and I study every situation I enter. Doing this gives me an edge that allows me to step into the realm of a woman's mind that her last boyfriend didn't even know existed.

To be a certified MAC means you have a Masters degree in Communicating. You know how to listen; just as well as what to say, and when to say it. You watch the body language, and can recognize the subtle clues that women telegraph through their words and mannerisms. Being a MAC is extremely necessary in your trek to seduction. Not every woman is the same. Women are deep, but that doesn't have to make them complicated. As you delve deeper into this book I'll switch gears into face to face Mackin', but I'm taking my time getting there because I realize that there's different levels to the game.

At the end of this chapter I've included a number of poems. You can use them like you want; poems are poems. I use 'em at the beginning of each letter I send out. Every letter I write a woman includes some type of poem, or quote, or words of wisdom at the beginning. I do it to set the tone, I also do it because it takes up space and allows me the option to cut the missive short if I got too much on my plate that night.

No one ever said being a MAC was easy. This is a job, playboy. You get what you put in. When you start accumulating a harem— you'll get busy. You'll be writing all day, every day. The minute you slack off, your females will start falling off. That's why the material in this book is so important. Just think of every pre–written letter, poem, song, etc., as heat/firepower/bullets/missles. What I do is every time I use one of these poems
— I'll write the name and date of what girl I sent it to next to the poem. This keeps me from sending the same poem to the same woman.

In my book How to Hustle and Win: Sex, Money, Murder Edition, I have a chapter called Play Ya' Position. That essay was geared towards niggaz in the game. For this stage I want to flip the script and present a different point of view on that same subject...

The "basic" inmate sees a female pen pal as a possible source of money. Real talk, there's no beating around bushes in my books. I call these cats "basic" because there's no high definition to their vision. I'm not a "basic nigga," and I'm not an inmate either. I'm cut from some expensive, imported cloth— meaning the things I've seen and/or done are above average.

There are inmates who will find out a pen pal has no money to give and they'll immediately decide to discard her. I can't do that. I'm a firm believer that everyone has a position to play. When I was younger, one of my mentors taught me that I should have a female to meet/fulfill each of my five basic needs:

Financial/Sexual/Commercial/Emotional/Residential

I took that game and applied it to this prison shit. The game don't stop. It doesn't matter where you're from... It's all about where you're at.

Let me tell you some T.R.U.T.H. about the majority of today's prison population. The average inmate wasn't just arrested, he was rescued. A lot of these guys have never had their own spot where they had to pay bills. Most of these imaginary ballers were in–the–way on the streets. So they have a distorted view when it comes to the finances of a female civilian. And this limits their vision, thus limiting their opportunities.

Listen, y'all, I got one pen pal who runs my social media. She got me posted on Facebook, Instagram and Twitter so much, that even when I'm in the hole you'd think I still got my cell phone. I have another pen pal who doesn't send money (or write) but she'll answer all my collect calls and make 3–ways for me. I have a pen pal who doesn't send money, but she loves taking pussy–flicks for ya' boy. Yes, I do have a Queen who looks out for me financially, but baby is a Boss Bitch who is in a position to meet those needs head–on. Not everyone has it like that. I understand this and it's fine with me.

Another thing I want to talk about is "shelf–life." There is a train of thought that teaches convicts to be gorillas on females because, according to this notion, they all eventually leave so you gotta get everything you can while you can. Basically, the idea is that females who ride with prisoners are good for 1–3 years, then they're gone no matter what you do.

It would be a fraudulent statement for me to say that females don't bounce. They do, that's life. You're not guaranteed to stay with any woman for 1–3 years on the streets. Just think how much harder it is to keep her when you can't protect, provide or penetrate her rectum. This shit is deep... But that doesn't necessarily mean they all live on the same timeline.

If you think like that, you'll start to act and talk like that. And women can sense these things. I'm not telling you to be unrealistic, what I am telling you is to shape your game along the lines of where you want it to be.

Have you ever heard the adage: Dress for the job you want, not the one you got. That's real talk; but you gotta elevate it and apply it to your daily mathematics. Instead of treating these women like they're a nut–rag, put it in your mind that she's gonna ride with you for the next ten years. Think longevity. Recognize and utilize her assets, at the same time pace yourself.

For example: If you know who's willing to spend $500 on a package, get her to commit to spending that much. Then, right when the time comes for you to send her a list, send her a $300 list instead. When she asks what happened to the $500, tell her you thought about her and you didn't want her to spend all that when you know that she has bills to pay... Bruh, don't trip, you'll get the remaining dividends when the time comes.

Pace yourself. Think positive. With the right game plan, you can prolong that alleged shelf life.

POEMS

Moments in Life...

There are moments in life when you miss someone so much that you just want to pick them from your dreams and hug them for real!!! When the door of happiness closes, another opens. Yet, oftentimes we don't see the one that opens because we are caught up in the rapture of uncertainty. Don't go for physical beauty, even that fades. Go for someone who makes you smile, because a smile can make a dark day bright and worth while. Find that one person who has the ability to make your heart smile. Dream what you want to dream, go where you want to go, be what you want to be because you only live once (YOLO), thus you only get this one chance to live.

May you have enough happiness to make you sweet, enough trials to make you strong, enough sorrow to keep you humble, and enough hope to keep you happy. B.U.T.

knowledge this: The happiest of people don't have to be the best at everything. They just make the best of every opportunity that comes their way. The brightest future will always be based on a forgotten past. You can't go forward in life until you let go of your past failures, mistakes and heartbreaks.

And one more thing... Never count the years count the memories! Life isn't measured by the number of breaths we take, but by the moments that take our breath away...

$$\$\$\$\$\$$$

Memories
by Douglas R.A. Mack

I often wonder as I stroll
Why do I know what I know
What life on earth do we seek
Before time places us beneath
What do we have when all our friends are gone
What seems to make life linger on
The events which we all recall
As our minds just seem to stall
When in meditation I sit still
I assure that I am not ill
But need the bliss of solitude
To bolster my waning fortitude
I still remember the hurricane
That ruined my house with wind and rain
The youthful days of school and play
We enjoyed so much in every way
As we grow from childhood to adulthood
What follows us in every place we stood
As time now unravels these mysteries
I see clearly now that it's our memories

$$$$$

Life is a song
Sing it!
Life is a game
Play it!
Life is a challenge... Meet it!
Life is a dream... Realize it!
Life is a sacrifice... Offer it!
Life is love... Enjoy it!

$$$$$

You're a diamond in the rough
A jewel in the wild
A precious star in the sky
A moon with a smile
You are my treasure

$$$$$

Struggle

Knowing nothing less I push to my limits,
Working hard at everything I do so therefore I must finish.
No gimmicks. Raw Talent. Pure, one–hundred percent uncut.
I'm on the rise using all will power and no luck.
Everything I touch is beautiful, marvelous, one of a kind.
Mired in heart, soul and sweat. Not easy to find.
Some become blind to the harsh truths and bold facts.
Of my past and let my work now record my tracks.
Perhaps my fight inspires the spirit to commit change,
So if lives are transformed because of it, I'd love to be blamed.

Cause chains no longer hold me back, or keep me tied down.
My demons I defeated, look sad and all wear a frown.
I found in life you push forward in yourself. Continue to believe.
No matter what other mind and eyes may otherwise perceive,
Continue on knees and know that change will come in prayer.
Breaking us down, top to bottom, layer by layer.
A team player, I am, I know because I'm always in the huddle.
Even with change... it doesn't matter, it never stops the struggle.

$$\$\$\$\$\$$

Relapsed

I'm an addict in recovery, taking one day at a time,
Looking in the mirror for something that is hard to find.
No longer do I shine, I'm dull, taking the 1st step of 12.
Heart heavy, living in fear, yet I refuse to accept failure.
Been through hell, a trail that many of us can trace.
I don't want no more, it's time for me to face the facts,
Replace heartache with something else.
No one can do it for me... I must do it myself!
Remembering how I felt. I say I will love no more.
So I lock the lock and throwaway the key to my heart's door.
Not keeping score, but my wins are at none.
Life can't be this hard, there has to be someone.
Hold on... Here she comes! How'd she do it? Picked the lock with a smile.
Smart, sexy, cool, her conversation drives me wild.
Style like no other, my glow is back in place,
She's god–loving, god–fearing, me being the same,
I can relate. Soulmate, could this really mean I'm back on track?
Love is my drug of choice... Looks like I just relapsed.

$$$$$

Smile... You're beautiful

Never mind the cover, look inside.
Full of love, care and vision— hard to find.
Divine and heavenly, bright as the sun.
Words of wisdom always on the tongue.
Desire sprung, searching seeking for more,
On the wings of an angel, my spirit soars.
Ready to explore, my thoughts are always on you,
Knowing that... Smile... You're beautiful.

$$$$$

Time to think...

When I think I think about Love.
I think about support.
I think about rare moments.
I think about beauty.
I think about strength.
Above all, I think I think about... YOU!

$$$$$

Meant to be

Here I am on this sleepless night.
I pick up my pen and begin to write.
To my wife, a beautiful poem about love.
About how it's stronger than any bear hug.
Can't be budged, not even a lil' bit.
Forged by god so nothing can cripple it.

66

A connection made that will never be broken.
I confess my love in more ways than just spoken.
I was hoping you believe in every word I say.
To protect and to save you, my life I would say.
A price I would pay, for our love is so strong.
Because there's life after death and our love carries on.
Proving wrong— those who thought we wouldn't last.
As they watch us grow and the years go past.
Baby, my task is to give all of me till the last drop.
I can't be bought, gift wrapped in any kind of shop.
I'm at the top, there's nothing better than this.
Heart, mind, body and soul, all of it you'll get.
Take a trip, go on a journey and give in to ecstasy.
But, wrapped in my arms you'll be, cuz we were meant to be...

$$$$$

Find Me

To find me all it'll take is one simple look,
My design is unique one of a kind, no text book.
No nook or cranny will you find me in.
I'm close to you, I'm more than a friend.
We started out slow, but now feel the rush,
Truth be told you can feel me without a touch.
I stand tall, but will lay down for you if I have to,
enduring all kinds of pains and hurts only for you.
Still no clue? I cost and yet I'm free.
I'm in, I'm out, I'm all about, here for you to find me!
Find me, I'm the truth and can only be hurt by lies.
I stand out on purpose, since I refuse to wear a disguise.
In the eye, I'm that sparkle giving you delight,
Like wings on an angel soaring into flight.
I renew life and give the hopeless hope.
Who am I that heals hearts that are broke?

I'm no court gesture, yet I'm cool to be around,
though I've suffered a lot nothing can keep me down.
Sometimes lost, sometimes found, I'm a rare sight made of
beauty.
I AM LOVE, and I want you to come find me!

$$$$$

Power of Words

From my lips I speak nothing but the truth,
In a calm voice, or even shouted from a roof.
I've no troops, yet my words are said with the force of an army,
I'm captivated by the way you charm me.
Our harmony is like the lyrics to a song,
Feeling so good that it has to be wrong.
Strong and still so soft to a touch,
That even though I'm locked up, I still feel strong.
When I'm locked down, I still feel up.
Standing on this square with you I can't lose,
others see yet are still confused.
Never used to bruise your heart or soul,
I even feel safe giving you total control.
From the cold world I'll keep you warm,
Whatever life throws at us we'll get through the storm.
Remember the thorns don't take the beauty from the rose,
And the past is behind us, so bring it to a close.
God knows my love for you runs deep,
From my head to my toes, body and soul.
You're my peak my very mountain top,
Feelings so strong, on my knees I drop.
As you watch and nothing is disturbed,
I'm verbally confessing my love for you in these powerful
words...

$$$$$

Patience

When I wake, I taste you on my tongue... I inhale your scent.
And, in the back of my mind we lay on silken sheets to explore each other's lips.
We mingle and exist outside of all frames of time, so I'm patient with our love making. Your rhythm matches with mine, your softness on my hardness, your wetness drowns my dry. Your soft moans reach my ears and send some past the visible sky.
An addiction that corrupts us both more than any high.
A dream for now it may seem, or maybe a fantasy... I'd like to look at it as a prediction. We'll just have to wait and see... have patience.

$$$$$

It's our Anniversary...

What god has brought together no man can tear apart,
from spark to flame love burns inside your heart.
Being smart is how you must remain,
Remember the old, but revel in your change.
Strains in our union are sure to come,
But in life adversity is something we can't run from.
You're my earth and I'm your sun, please understand,
No one's plans are far brighter or better than yours,
So we gonna strive for success as we explore
Ups and downs, joy and pain.
Storing memories all over again.
Fame or nothing at all share a love that's fast,
YOLO... living everyday as if it's our last.
And with our seeds we'll leave a legacy of royalty.

Baby, I love you... It's our Anniversary.

$$$$$

My Ten Best Promises

1. I promise to always love you.
2. I promise to have fun with you.
3. I promise to admit when I'm wrong,
4. I promise to respect you.
5. I promise to trust you.
6. I promise to give you freedom and space.
7. I promise to worry about you.
8. I promise to always forgive you.
9. I promise to help you find your dreams, and let you live them!
10. And finally... I promise to be here for you... Always right here!

$$$$$

Smile

Remember life happens faster than it seems.
And life is hard, every struggle, every obstacle... makes you wanna scream!
But we find that with it, joy does appear.
Giving us the strength to face all of our fears.
We hold dear these moments of success,
These are the moments we're at our best.
Don't stress when life seems to keep you down,
just remember, only you can turn it around.
So, round after round, put up a fight it'll be better in lil' while.
And these are the times I look forward to the most,
Because with every victory comes a beautiful smile!

$$$$$

Life is a Balancing Act

Work... Home
Family. .. Friends
Self... Others
Spend it... Save it
Hold on... Let go
Fast... Slow
Just remember, whether it's smiles or frowns, ups or downs, give or take... It's bound to even out. So hang in there and believe in yourself!

$$$$$

For Me...

For me... You must believe that nothing remains the same, known in your heart that troubled times will leave, it's the cause of change.
For me... Remember my love and know that it will return to you, know that without a doubt, all that I do I do it for you.
For me... Don't worry or stress so much, know that soon I will ease all of your pain with a simple touch.
For me... Be happy and glad at all times, know that it could be worse, but on your face the sun always shines.
For me... Only for me, think about the last time I made you smile, now that good things come in just a lil' while.
For me talk and listen to your heart, know that I'll be there for you.
For me (Name), our prison is nothing. I'll get released, know that I love you and Please put your mind at ease... if only just for me...

$$$$$

For You...

For you... My love grows stronger with each passing day, I know that it's me for who you patiently wait.
For you... I will face any trial head–up and head–on, I know that my desire for you is just that strong.
For you... My life has really changed, trust and believe that. I know you are the one for me, just simply stating facts.
For you... I do things that I thought were impossible for me. And I know this isn't all talk, baby, you'll see.
For you... God has brought me this far, I know things could've been worse—I've seen the death of a star.
For you... I ignore ignorance, work hard, keep my mind on my release. I know I must stay strong, and avoid wrong. My love, you are my Peace!
For you... I faithfully make my body, which is your body, fit and lean. I know all the things you desire me to be.
For you... I am ready to show and prove my love is true, and I know that you love me too, this is why I thank god for you!

$$$$$

When I Miss You (Just in case you're wondering)

I miss you when I'm by myself instead of where you are...
I miss you when I'm all alone and driving my car...
I miss you when you're someplace else and I've got thoughts to share...
I miss you when I'm on the couch by myself...
I miss you when I need a hug and you are not around.
I miss you when our busy schedules keep us separated
I miss you when I'm in the mood and you're not around

I miss you when I'm with a friend and not with you
I miss you when you're out of town or not with me
I miss you when you're anywhere instead of with me

I miss you...

$$$$$

Someone is You

Someone that is there for you no matter what.
Someone that can ease the pain with the slightest touch.
Someone who cares and gives nothing but love.
Someone who seeks guidance from the lord above.
Someone special who is the apple of my eye.
Someone who when I'm down helps me get by.
Someone you can count on even when you've done wrong.
Someone who sticks to you and helps you stand strong.
Someone who knows the way when you're lost.
Someone who has seen a lot and knows the meaning of loss.
Someone who brings joy on any given day.
Someone who is lovely and always knows what to say.
Someone who is a bright light on the darkest night.
Someone who is soft and sweet, but ready for a fight.
Someone who is always ready to use love as a guide.
Someone who is down to ride, never switch sides.
Someone who has my heart and is one with my soul.
Someone who knows no limits, and beauty's to behold.
Someone you should cherish with all that's in you.
Someone who in a time of need knows exactly what to do.
Someone who's ahead of her time always divine.
Someone who's been around, yet still in her prime.
Someone who say my barriers and came crashing through.
Someone tried and true, that someone is YOU!

$$$$$

Forever

Until the end of time... Tell me, what does that mean?
See, I only thought that it existed only in movies and dreams.
I know about beautiful things such as love and passions.
I think I'm on the brink of something, therefore I'm asking.
No masking, there's part of me that I want to live on.
The part that shows my best healthy and strong.
That's why I long to let you know exactly how I feel.
If I were a professional burglar, your heart is what I'd steal.
I'd make a sinful deal just to continue to hear your laugh,
such a joyful sound that's in its own distinctive class.
You're my other half and, baby, I want you to know,
You're my water, it's you that nurtures my growth.
Together we flow like streams in heaven, gentle and smooth.
Lovely is your make–up, rare, natural… nothing to prove.
I choose to believe that this is destiny, it means this is great,
Like the description of angels standing before heaven's gate.
Now, take a look at my face, see the formation of a grin,
the answer came to me, no longer can I pretend.
Time will never end, in fact it's very clever.
I finally realized that time created love and love last forever.

$$$$$

I Love You

You are an angel in my eyes,
A gift from God, a wonderful surprise.
Hypnotized is how you keep me,
Every minute, hour, day… even weekly.
Deeply are my feelings that I express,
Never bored with you, I need no rest.

I confess, you turn my grey skies blue.
Your smile, your laugh, lil' things you do.
This makes me pursue happiness just to give it to you.
It'll be wrapped in my heart, hope you feel it too.
No limit to the things I'll do, just so you'll know how deeply I
love you.

$$$$$

When Love Walked In...

Love walked right in and
Drove the shadows away.
Love walked right in and
Brought my sunniest day.
One magic moment and
My heart seemed to know
That love said... hello,
though, not a word was spoken.
One look and I forgot
The gloom of the past;
One look and I had
Found my future at last.

$$$$$

When things go wrong as they sometimes will;
When the road you're trudging seems all uphill;
When the funds are low and the debts are high;
And you want to smile but you have to sigh;
When care is pressing you down a bit;
Rest if you must, but don't quit.
Life is queer with its twists and turns;
As every one of us sometimes learns;
And many a failure turns about;

When you might have won had you stuck it out.
Don't give up though the pace seems slow;
You may succeed with another blow.
Success is failure turned inside out;
The silver tint of the clouds of doubt;
And you never can tell how close you are;
An army can be near when it seems so far; So stick to the fight
when you're hardest hit...
It's when things seem worst,
That you must not quit!

$$$$$

I Just Wanna Touch

I just wanna touch you in every single place,
Beauty can't replace so I must start at your face.
Trace along the lines of your beautiful eyes,
Simply divine, full of love, the motor of our lives.
Wonderful to the eyes, graceful is your nose to your lips,
An electrifying sensation flowing through me from my
fingertips.
I continue my trip down your shoulders to your breast,
Nice and firm, tell me, can you feel my caress?
And I confess, gliding across your stomach lovely is your skin,
I don't ever wanna stop, I hope you can comprehend.
As I begin my journey to the sweet center of you,
every warm, preciously moist fold, are you real? Is this true?
I know your wondering too? Moving to your thighs and your
calves,
Thick and lovely in every single way, and that's just the half.
I may drag for a moment on your pretty, tender feet,
Putting goddesses to shame, I swear, baby, this is deep.
Making angels weep as I reach out to your soul,
Hoping to come in contact is my one main goal.

And having full contact, I hope I'm not asking for too much,
But with words right now, it's your heart I just wanna touch...

$$$$$

Your Smile

It's like a cool breeze on a summer night,
A reason to pull you closer and hold you tight.
A wonderful sight, pure beauty to behold,
My treasure... more valuable than silver and gold.
Truth be told I love you more than life,
Precious is the soul of my soon to be lovely wife.
We're getting it right, share a bond like no other.
Close like a baby in the womb of its mother,
Smother with love that was meant to be.
I know when I look upon your face and see
what was meant for me, and makes my heart melt.
Makes me feel the way I never once felt.
Yourself alone have made the impossible happen,
On the rough sea of love, the first female captain.
Heart clapping and beating fast because of you.
You're the reason I smile, no need to feel blue.
And it's true, the first to get me sprung,
Nose wide open and love filled lungs.
How was it done? make me walk a country mile,
I don't know the reason, so I blame it on your smile.

$$$$$

Love Is

Love is... more than just hearts and flowers and romance
more than candle lit dinners and dancing.
More than walks in the park and moments of intimate sharing.

Something that lasts beyond the initial stages.
Understanding through the difficult times.
Caring past the disagreements.
Laughing together when things are good, or laughing together to keep from crying when things couldn't seem to go more wrong.
Patience and compassion, compromise and healing.
Also forgiving and forgiving and forgiving.
Everything we share together, because to me, love is and always will be YOU!

$$$$$

The Rose

The petals are the softness of your skin and the tenderness of your heart.
The leaves are times that will come and go.
In tension, that will part the thorns are the pain we'll go through and still survive.
The stem is the strength and foundation that keeps our love alive.
The scent of the rose is the sweetness of our character.
The bud that replenishes itself is the everlasting love and life that two can share.
This emotion of love is energy–in–motion and it can truly be.
I'd be blessed if you'd share it with me.

$$$$$

I'm Gone

Would anyone put on my shoes for a day,
missing your lover, in desperate need of word play.
Or, should I ask what about your lover's touch?

78

Even the smile that brings joy to your heart so much?
It's a rush to hear the voice of the person you love,
wishing with all you got for a chance to hug.
Or, rub the beautiful face and kiss the tender lips.
It'll block out the moon and make the sun eclipse.
How would you feel if it was all taken away?
Imagine that pain in the course of one day.
Now, I say, I wouldn't give anyone such a task.
Can you picture a face with tears for a permanent mask?
All I ask is that you always pick up that phone, and the best
reason in the world is that I'm gone...

$$$$$

Everlasting Love

You are my love, my life and my future...
The love I feel is for no one but you.
Things that were important to me have become secondary.
I long for your company, your touch and your warm embrace.
Each day begins with thoughts of you,
And ends with dreams of you.
You are everything to me!
My love, my life and my future,
With you, my life filled with promise; I love you...

$$$$$

My Promise

I promise to give you the best of my love, and to ask of you
no more than you can give.
I promise to accept you the way you are. I fell in love with you
for the qualities, abilities and outlook on life that you have,
and I won't try to reshape you into another image.

I promise to respect you as a person with your own intent, destiny and needs and to realize that those are sometimes different, but no less important than my own.
I promise you my all.
I promise to share with you my time, my close attention and to bring joy, strength and imagination to our relationship.
I promise I will keep myself open to you, to let you see through the window of my personal world... into my innermost fears, and feelings, secrets and dreams.
I promise to grow along with you, to be willing to face changes as we both evolve in order to keep our relationship alive and exciting. And finally, I promise to love you in good times and bad times with all I have to give and all I feel inside, in the only way I know how, completely and forever!!!

$$$$$

As We Dance Within The Midnight Flames!!

Midnight now, your eyes, like candles luring,
Flicker with seduction, and I a moth,
Burn! Burn! in lust fires softly stirring,
Wrapped–up and slowly consumed as an oily cloth.

Living gems; your eyes compel yet quench me,
as willingly I linger in their blaze
To prove my love, in carnal purgatory:
Waiting, craving, melting into your gaze.

Now feed the furnace: bait me with a kiss
Your mouth is so wet (a douse of kerosene...)
I burst my chains, unable to resist,
Lips on lips, soft skin, you lurid sheen.

And as we dance within the midnight flames,

With eyes to eyes and flesh of flesh transfixed,
Incinerations doubts, and fears and shames,
Our passion and our hearts are intermixed.

Our souls together merge in conflagration,
Twining limbs in ecstasies, untamed.
Unrestrained, in long sought consummation,
Thrusting, groaning, and sweaty and inflamed!

Now the climax comes— now I awake...
The dream, unfinished, leaves me to myself.
I rise to calm my nerves, and up I take
My photographs from resting on their shelf.

My fingers stroke the image of your face,
As I confess the things I feel for you.
I kiss your pictures, put them back in place,
Return to bed, and dream the dream anew.

$$$$$

Why I Love You

I love you because you're the only person who has me in mind, body and soul.

I love you because you have taught me how to take charge in my life through the power of first believing in myself.

I love you because you have made my life more colorful, exciting and alive by showing me that happiness isn't just being content. It's striving toward the desires in your heart until some part of it has been obtained.

I love you because you are that once in a life time person who has given me the chance of a lifetime to have a never ending stream of success in whatever I do.

I love you because you are the only person who has equally shared in helping me grow and learn how to live life and live more abundantly.

$$$$$

CHAPTER FOUR

SOCIAL MEDIA

In this chapter I want to discuss a technique that I picked up on by accident. I call this section "Social Media" because of the avenues I'll be discussing, yet it might not be how you think I'm gonna use them. A lot of guys use Facebook and Instagram to reach out to females and network. That's actually a good idea; it works, it definitely works... but that's self–explanatory. If you got a phone in your cell I strongly recommend that you wake up every morning and map out your daily agenda before you get on. Instead of surfing the porn sites or watching the latest YouTube video, get on some dating sites and crack you some women. Log onto all those "free" pen pal websites and post your profile on 'em. Touch base with females you lost contact with over the years. All that is being on point. But that's still not what I'm about talk about. There's so much more to social media than the basic shit, and most of the time, as a prisoner, your access is limited so you want to utilize your resources to the highest level possible.

I've learned to utilize my social media websites as more of a reference tool for my pen pals. What I do is (through a pen pal, family member, or friend) I post all kinds of positive quotes, thoughts, or messages every chance I get. I post all my pictures, too. I do this so whenever I do meet someone new I can send her to my Facebook page and she'll have all kinds of information about me that she can process for herself.

The best thing about this technique is I have created a specific persona that "I" approve of. And so can you! Anyone who has done any substantial amount of time knows that prison is a place where you can recreate yourself. The majority of the guys in here lie about half the shit they were doing on the streets. And unless there's someone from their area to dispute their fantastic stories of grandeur, you may never know the truth. The internet is the same way.

If you want to make yourself seem like a hopeless romantic — post love poems. If you want to make yourself look socially conscious, post entries about current events. The internet is a blank slate for you to draw on, and once you've created a specific landscape you can send people there for them to come to their own conclusion about who "you" are.

And here's where it gets deep: You don't have to stop at Facebook or Twitter. Have you ever heard of a website called PrisonsFoundation.org? This website publishes inmate books for free. It doesn't matter whether it's typed or written by hand, they'll publish anything you send them (as is) on their website so anyone can read your manuscript free of charge.

I've got several books published on that website right now. And I send everyone I meet to that site so they can read my books. The books I have there aren't urban novels either. They're non–fiction. They are philosophical and biographical in nature. So anyone who takes the time to read them are offered the opportunity to glimpse into my mental. Since I constantly write I have work on there that shows my artistic as well as an intellectual growth. [see PrisonsFoundation.org – Sex Money Murder by Wilberto Belardo and Plus Lessons From The Interior Cipher by Wilberto Belardo]

I have also written articles for Bay View Newspaper amongst other prison friendly publications. Everything I do can be found through a quick google search. Now, these may not be traditional pen pal profiles geared towards pulling a female, but my work on social media shows my drive and passion to network. So when a new pen–friend checks it all out, she can see for herself that I'm not a bottom–feeder who is sitting in prison wasting his time.

I guess what I'm telling you in this chapter is to use social media to create a digital footprint. Also, something I've realized is that, especially with Facebook, certain people will watch your progress without you even realizing it. For instance; I was estranged with one of my baby mammas for years. I wrote about my ex–wife in my How to Hustle and Win: Sex Money Murder Edition book. Baby was in the game with me when shit was hectic. She pulled away from me because of the lifestyle we were in was too dangerous to raise a child in. She wouldn't even accept the money I would send her when I was out. But last summer (after ten years of no communication) she contacted me. She had been monitoring my social media sites, and after convincing herself that I had changed she decided to finally get at me. And now I'm in contact with my daughter and we're building a beautiful relationship.

So, keep all that in mind when you get access to the internet. Whether you can post things yourself, or you utilize a pen pal to do it— take advantage of all of your opportunities. Think ahead, and think before you post. Most of the shit you put out there will stay out there for years to come...

Oh, yeah, here's some song lyrics for you to add with your missives. Sometimes, all it takes is a few lines from a specific song to spice up a love letter.

Gone Till November
lyrics by Wyclef Jean

I dedicate this record the carnival to all you brothas takin' long trips
Down South, Virginia, Baltimore, all around the world

And your girls get this message that you ain't coming back
She sittin' back in her room, da lights is off
She's cryin', and then my voice comes in Pow!
And in the middle of the night and this what I tell her for you

[chorus]

Every time I make a run, girl you turn around and cry
I ask myself why, oh why?
See, you must understand I can't work a 9 to 5
So I'll be gone till November

[chorus]

Said I'll be gone till November, I'll be gone till November
You tell my girl I'll be gone till November I'll be gone till November
I'll be gone till November, You tell my girl I'll be gone till November

[chorus]

January, February, March, April, May
I see you cryin' but girl I can't stay I'll be gone till November, I'll be gone till November
And give a kiss to my mother
When I come back there be no time to clock
I'll have enough money to buy out the glocks
Tell my brother go to school in September
So he won't mess up in summer school in da summer

Tell my cousin Jerry wear his condom
If you don't wear a condum you see a red line
Oh, you sucka M.C.'s you got no flo
I heard ya style, you so, so

(chorus)
(chorus)
(chorus)

I had to flick nothin' and turn it in to somethin,
Hip–hop turns to the future of rock when I smash a pumpkin
Commit treason now I have a reason
To hunt you down its only right, its rappers season, Yeah you

With the loud voice posing like you're top choice
I make a hertz out of ya Rolls Royce
Besides, I got my girl to remember
I committed to that, I'll be gone till November

(chorus)
(chorus)
(chorus)

I know the hustle's hard, but we gotta enterprise, the carnival

$$\$\$\$\$\$$$

The Beginning
lyrics by John Legend

Last night was the last night
You'll ever spend alone
Couldn't wait
Did it in the living room
Soon as I saw you, baby, I had plans
Plans to do it till we have a baby
 Even if the world is crazy
Pick some names, boy or girl
Then we'll change, change the world

[chorus]

So after you change your clothes
Girl, if you change your mind
I'm ready, whatever time

[chorus]

It's the beginning of forever
You don't have to go
Sometimes you just know
It's the beginning forever
It don't have to end
Keep doing it, and doing it again, oh
Keep doing it. and doing it again, oh
Last time was the last time I was one and done
You the best, that's why I want another one
Soon as I saw you, baby, I had plans
Planned to take you to my elevator
And cook a little breakfast later
Pick a place and go there, girl
Then we'll change, change the world

(chorus)
(chorus)

$$$$$

Best Man
lyrics by Jagged Edge

Tell me what's the reason
That a man's own woman could be so cold
And tell me how the two of you could do

What you were doin right in my home
We were supposed to get married
It's kinda scary that we just almost did
I hope that you're happy 'cuz you got each other
I don't know part of your love

[chorus]

You were my best man
She meant everything to me
She was my girlfriend
Closer than two could ever be
You were my best man, best man, yeah
yeah Supposed to be my best friend

Should've known when I asked a question
You couldn't even look me in my eyes no more
Then you st–st–stutter
Talkin' bout some "You know better", man hell no, no
Tell me how could you, you
Forget about the situation that we've been through
Tell me why? oh why? why?
Did you cheat on me, baby, baby, tell me why?

Think about the time
Thinking bout all the time we shared
Together you and I
I remember when you were my best friend
What's the reason?
What's the reason why, why, why? Why, why, why, why,
why?

(chorus)
(chorus)
(chorus)

$$$$$

If Only For One Night
lyrics by Luther Vandross

[chorus]

Let me hold you tight
If only for one night
Let me keep you near
To ease away your fear
It would be so nice
If only for one night

I won't tell a soul
No one has to know
If you want to be totally discreet
I'll be at your side
If only for one night
Your eyes say things I never hear from you
And my knees are shakin' too
But I'm willin' to go thru
I must be crazy
Standin' in this place
But I'm feeling no disgrace

For asking...

(chorus)
I tell you what I need is
On night, one night, oh (and oh, oh)
What I need is One night, one night
Of your love, of you love, of your loving ooh
I'm asking...

Let me take you home
To keep you safe and warm
Till the early dawn
Warms up to the sun
It would be so nice if only for one night
If only for one night
If only for one night
If only for one night, night, night —yeah one night
If only for one... night

$$$$$

Crazy Love
lyrics by Brian McKnight

I can hear her heartbeat from a thousand miles
Hear the heavens open every time she smiles
And when I come to her like a river strong

[chorus]

She gives me love, love, love, love, crazy love
She gives me love, love, love, love, crazy love

She got a fine sense of humor when I'm feeling low down
And when I come home to her when the sun goes down
Take my troubles all away, take away my grief
Take away my heartache, in the night like a thief

(chorus)

Yes, I need, Yes, I need her in the daytime
And. oh I need, yes, I need her in the night
I want to throw my arms all around her

To kiss and hug· and kiss and hug her tight and, oh

And when I'm returning from so far away
She gives me sweet, sweet leavin' brighten up my day
It makes me righteous and it makes me whole
Makes me mellow, down into my soul

(chorus)

One more time, she gives me love, lust a lil' love
When I wake up in the morning
She gives me love, love, crazy, crazy love

$$$$$

Don't Take The Girl
lyrics by Tim McGraw

Johnny's daddy was takin' him fishin'
When he was eight years old
A little girl came through the front gate
Holdin' a fishin' pole

His dad looked down and smiled
Said, "We can't leave her behind
Son, I know you don't want her to go
But someday you'll change you mind."

And Johnny said
"Take Jimmy Johnson
Take Tommy Thompson
Take my best friend Bo."

"Take anybody that you want
As long as she don't go

Take any boy in the world
Daddy, please don't take the girl."

Same old boy, same sweet girl
Ten years down the road
He held her tight and kissed her lips
In front of the picture show

Stanger came and pulled a gun
Grabbed her by the arm
Said, "If you do what I tell you to
There won't be any harm."

And Johnny said
Take my money
Take my wallet
Take my credit cards.

Here's the watch that my grandma gave me
Here's the key to my car
Mister, give it a whirl
But, please don't take the girl."

Same old boy, same sweet girl
Five years down the road
There's gonna be a little one
And she says it's time to go

Doctor says
The baby's fine
But you'll have to leave
Cause his momma's
fadin' fast."

And Johnny hit his knees

And there he prayed
Take the very breath you gave me
Take the heart from my chest.

I'll gladly take her place if you'll let me
Make this my last request
Take me outta this world
God, please don't take the girl.
Johnny's daddy
was takin' him fishin'
when he was 8 years old...

$$$$$

The Best I Ever Had
lyrics by Drake

You know, a lot of girls be thinking my songs are about them
But this is not to get confused, this one's for you, baby

[chorus]

You my everything, you all I ever wanted
We can do it big, bigger than you ever done it
You'll be up on everything, other hoes ain't ever on it
I want this forever, I swear I can spend whatever on it
Cause she held me down every time I hit her up
When I get right I promise we gonna live it up
She made me beg for it 'till she give it up
And I say the same thing every single time
I say you the fuckin' best

[chorus]

You the fuckin' best. You the fuckin' best,

You the fuckin' best. You the fuckin' best I ever had,
best I ever had, best I ever had.
I say you the fuckin' best...

Know you got a roommate, call me when there's no one there
Put the key under the mat, you know I'll be over there (Yup!)
I'll be over there shorty, I'll be over there
I'll be hittin all the spots that you ain't even know was there
And you don't ever have to ask twice
You can have my heart or we can share it like the last slice
Always felt like you was so accustomed to the fast life
Have a nigga thinking that he met you in a past life
Sweatpants, hair tied, chillin with no make–up on
That's when you're the prettiest, I hope that you don't take it
wrong
You don't even trip when friends say you ain't bringing Drake
along
You know that I'm working, I'll be there as soon as I make it
home
And she patient in my waiting room

Never pay attention to the rumors and what they assume And
until them girls prove it, I'm the one to never get confused wit'
Cause, baby you my everything

(chorus)

(chorus)

Sex, love, pain, baby I be on that Tank shit
Buzz so big I could probably see a blank disk
When my album drops, bitches'll buy it for the picture
And niggas'll buy it too and claim they got it for their sister
Magazine, paper, girl, but money ain't the issue
They bring dinner to my room and ask me to initial

95

She call me "The referee" cause I be so official
My shirt ain't got no stripes but I can make your pussy whistle
Like the Andy Griffin theme son, and who told you to put
them jeans on?
Double cup, love, you the one I can lean on
Feelin for a fix then you should really get your fiend on
Yeah, just know my condo is the crack spot
Every single show she out there reppin' like a mascot
Get it from the back and make your fuckin' bra strap pop
All up in your slot till a nigga hit the jackpot

(chorus)

(chorus)

$$\$\$\$\$\$$

Me and My Bitch
lyrics by Notorious B.I.G.

Yo, let, let me ask you a question, yo
Yo, would you kill for me?
(her) Hmm, yeah
What took you so long to answer mothafucka?
(her) I don't know
The fuck wrong with you, bitch?

When I first met you I admit my first thoughts was to trick
You look so good, huh, I suck on your daddy's dick
I never felt that way in my life
It didn't take long before I made you my wife
Got no rings and shit, just my main squeeze
Come into the crib, even had a set a keys

During the days you helped me bag up my nickels

In the process, I admit, I tricked a little
But you was my bitch, the one who'd never snitch
Love me when I'm broke or when I'm filthy rich
And I admit, when the time is right, the wine is right
I treat you right, you talk slick, I beat you right

[chorus]
Just me and my bitch
Just me and my bitch
Just me and my bitch

Moonlight strolls with the hoes, oh no, that's not my steelo
I wanna bitch that like to play celo, and craps
Packin' gats in a coach bag steamin' dime bags
A real bitch is all I want, all I ever had
With a glock just as strong as me

Totin' guns just as long as me, the bitch belongs with me
Any plans with another bitch, my bitch I'll spoil it
One day she used my toothbrush to clean the toilet

Throwin' my clothes out the windows, so when the wind
blows
I see my Polos and Timbos
Hide my car keys so I can't leave
A real slick bitch, keep a trick up her sleeve
And if I deceive, she won't take it lightly
She'll invite me, politely to fight G
And then we lie together, cry together I swear to God
I hope we fucking die together

(chorus)
(chorus)
(chorus)

She helped me plan out my robberies on my enemies
Didn't hesitate to squeeze, to get my life out of danger
One day she put 911 on the pager
Had to call back, whether its minor or major
No response, the phone just rung
Grab my vest, grab my gun to find out the problem
When I pulled up, police was on the scene
Had to make the u–turn, make sure my shit was clean

Drove down the block, trashed the burner in the bushes
Stepped to police with the shoves and the pushes
It didn't take long before the tears start
I saw my bitch dead with the gunshot to the heart
And when I find em your life is to an end
They killed my best friend, me and my bitch

(chorus)
(chorus)
(chorus)

$$\$\$\$\$\$$$

The Sweetest Love
lyrics by Robin Thicke

Why do people smile when no one's smiling?
It's cause they're thinking of someone they're loving
Keep on believing we are meant to be and
Nothing's stopping you and me from going to heaven
Sweetest love

[chorus]
I got the sweetest love there ain't nothing sweeter
I got the sweetest love there ain't nothing beatin' it
There ain't nothing sweeter

Now or never? Is about to inch just one ladder
 It gets better every second we're together
Oooh baby it feels so right
A new beginning starts tonight
The reason for when it's on
Is because of you and me
and Sweetest love

Finally I can't believe Cause you and me,
you're my sweetest love

(chorus)
(chorus)

Now I got that feeling in my gut
Now I need your fire in my life
Now I wanna give you love so much
And I keep on feeling my sweet, my sweet
Sweetest love
I can't believe you and me, we gotta be
You're my sweetest love

(chorus)
(chorus)
(chorus)

$$\$\$\$\$\$$

One Sweet Day
lyrics by Mariah Carey

Sorry I never told you
All I wanted to say
And now it's too late to hold you

'Cause you've flown away
So far away
Never had I imagined
Living without your smile
Feeling and knowing you hearing me
It keeps me alive

[chorus]
And I know you're shining down on me from heaven
Like so many friends we've lost along the way
And I know eventually we'll be together
One sweet day

Darling I never showed you
Assume you'd always be there
I took your presence for granted
But I always cared
And I miss the love we shared

(chorus)

Although the sun will never shine the same again
I'll always look to a brighter day
Lord, I know when I lay me down to sleep
You will always listen as I pray

(chorus)

Sorry I never told you
All I wanted to say

$$$$$

Come Close
lyrics by Common feat. Mary J. Blidge

[Common] It's just a fly love song, what
[Mary J] Mmmmm
[Common] It's just a fly love song, what

[Common]
Are we living in a dream world?
Are your eyes still green, girl?
I know you're sick and tired of arguing
But you can't keep it bottled in
Jealousy, we gotta swallow it
Your heart and mind, baby follow it
Smile, happiness you could model it
And when you feel opposite
I just want you to know
Your whole being is beautiful
I'ma do the best I can do
Cause I'm my best when I'm with you

[chorus] (Mary J)
Come close to me, baby
Let your love hold you
I know this world is crazy
What's it without you

[Common]
Put down your bags love
I know in the past love
Has been sort of hard in you
But I see the god in you
I just want to nurture it
Though this love may hurt a bit
We dealing wit' this water love

You even give my daughter love

101

I want to build a tribe wit' you
Protect and provide for you
Truth is I can't hide from you
The pimp in me
May have to die with you

(chorus)
[bridge]

I know what you're thinking, you're on my mind
You're right, you're right, you're right
You promise so fast you just might take flight
Hope you're not tired, tonight, tonight

[Common]
You help me to discover me
I just want you to put trust in me
I kind of laugh when you cuss at me
The aftermath is you touching me
It's destiny to we connected, girl
You and I we can affect the world
I'm tired of the fast lane
I want you to have my last night

(chorus)
(bridge)
(bridge)

CHAPTER FIVE

PERSEVERANCE

Regardless of where you choose to recruit women you have to learn how to be persistent. And it's gonna be hard, so that's where the perseverance comes in. You must keep trying, no matter how hard it gets... cuz it will get hard.

I've been on pen pal websites for a whole year without getting one hit. I've recently hit on one site (a free one) that I've been on for two and a half years! Or, I can go even longer if I count the sites that I've been on where I got pen pals, but didn't get anywhere with them. I've learned through experience that these things take time.

At the end of this chapter I've included a few jokes. Some cool shit you can add with your letters, or spit to a female in person. Women love to laugh; who doesn't? I could've listed a lot more jokes, but I didn't because it's not necessary. I give all my readers the credit they deserve. You know if I point you in a direction it must be worth something so you can look in that direction yourselves. What this means is if you read this essay and agree with me that adding jokes to your letters is a good thing, then you can go out there and look for more jokes on your own. The same goes for everything else I've been sharing y'all. Poems and songs are even better if you write them yourself...

I've got a folder and manila envelope where I stash my arsenal of poems and antidotes that I use in my letters. Yeah, I got a stash, everyone should. If you keep your arsenal all in one place you can pull it out every time you sit down to write a missive. It pays to be meticulous in your MAC'n. I named this section PERSERVERANCE because I don't want any of you to give up if things don't go your way right off the bat. Never give up! You might not hit on your first investment. Then again, you might... It help's not to put all your eggs in one basket, too. If you don't have the money to put yourself on a bunch of different websites, work with the free ones. They're just as good.

Now, I want to get into getting at the women around you. For a lot of years, in prison, I was anti–social when it came to staff. Especially the K9's. I would ignore them, and only speak to them when I was put in a situation where I needed to. It took me awhile, but I learned that I was missing out on too many opportunities. I've literally had a male K9 tell me that I gotta be blind cuz I acted like I didn't realize one of his co–workers was attracted to me.

It happens, but it's a different game than on the streets. In the free–world women choose–up a lot more than men realize. In prison, you need to give a female a reason to choose–up. You have to work harder than you did on the street and you can't give up when your advances are turned down.

Sometimes all it takes is a simple hello along with confident eye contact. It'll even work better when you take 2 seconds to read a name tag before approaching her. Whenever you call someone by their name it's a good thing because most people like hearing their name called out. Even in letters, I constantly start sentences with my pen pal's name.

Once you open that door with whomever you choose to get at, never let it close. Be in her face every chance you get. If it's a K9 who has to do count— stand at that door! If it's a kitchen staff— get a job! If it's a nurse— get on some meds!

Never let the next man tell you what you can or can't accomplish. I have to say this because if you're new to this shit, you'll forget that there's different levels to this shit. Not everyone is on what we're on. Not everyone is capable of accomplishing even the most elementary level of the game we're covering in this book. So, if you tell people what you want to accomplish with a woman, most of the time you'll get some sort of negative reception. They'll tell you it's not possible and all you're gonna do is get yourself in trouble. Or, the haters will say: "That lady got a job and she's free... what do she want with a convict?"

You can't let these basic–cats put a cloud over your thought process. If you entertain cats like that you'll begin to second guess yourself and that's a horrible thing because women can detect weakness real quick.

The catch is you gotta work hard at trying to pull a female in prison. No one ever said it was gonna be easy, that's why everyone isn't doing it. But anything is possible especially when you have a game plan in play. You might have five women turn down your advances (or, at least, seem to turn down your advances, but secretly smile at them) before one gives you play. That's just how it is in life.

Remember this: Everyone gets their time to shine. Everyone! If you miss your shot, it's on you. You're bad... If you're gonna be serious about cracking a woman then you have to live, breathe, eat and sleep with women on your mind.

So, back to these jokes. Some of them are dirty, and some women aren't into dirty jokes so watch yourself. But, putting them in your letters are always a great idea. And being able to tell 'em to someone in person is even better! Jokes are a tool of the trade. Everyone likes to laugh.

Surprise package

A man was drinking in a bar when he noticed this beautiful young lady sitting next to him. "Hello there," says the man, "and what is your name?"

"Hello," giggles the woman, "I'm Stacey. What's yours?"

"I'm Jim."

"Jim, do you want to come over to my house tonight? I mean, right now?"

"Sure!" replies Jim, "Let's go!"

So Stacey takes Jim to her house and takes him to her room. Jim sits down on the bed and notices a picture of a man on Stacey's desk. "Stacey, I noticed the picture of a man on your desk," Jim says.

"Yes? And what about it?" asks Stacey.

"Is it your brother?"

"No, it isn't, Jim!" Stacey giggles. Jim's eyes widen, suspecting that it might be Stacey's husband.

When he finally asks, "Is it your husband?"

Stacey giggles even more; "No; silly!" Jim was relieved.

"Then it must be your boyfriend!"

Stacey giggles even more while nibbling on Jim's ear. She says, "No, silly!"

"Then, who is it?" Jim asks.

Stacey replies, "That's me BEFORE my operation!"

$$$$$

The Penis

Request:

I the Penis hereby request a raise in salary for the following reasons...

1. I do physical labor

2. I work at great depths
3. I plunge head first into everything I do
4. I do not get weekends or public holidays off
5. I work in a damp environment
6. I do not get paid overtime
7. There is not any ventilation
8. I'm exposed to very high temperatures
9. I'm in danger of getting a contagious disease

Sincerely,
The Penis

Response:

After assessing your request and considering the arguments you raised, the administration REJECTS your request for the following reasons...

1. You do not work 8 straight hours
2. You often fall asleep after brief periods of work
3. You do not always follow orders from your management team
4. You refuse to stay in your designated work area
5. You are often found in RESTRICTED areas
6. You fail to take initiative and must be pressured and stimulated in order to start working
7. You leave your work place rather messy after each shift
8. You fail to comply with safety regulations, such as protective clothing
9. You will retire way before 65
10. You are physically unable to work double shifts
11. You have been known to leave your work area before completing your assigned tasks

AND IF THAT WEREN'T ENOUGH… YOU HAVE BEEN SEEN ENTERING AND LEAVING WORK CARRYING SUSPICIOUS LOOKING BAGS!!!

Sincerely,
The Management

$$$$$

A husband takes his wife to play her first game of golf. Of course, the wife promptly whacked her first shot right through the window of the biggest house adjacent to the course. The husband cringed, "I warned you to be careful! Now we'll have to go up there, find the owner, apologize and see how much your lousy drive is going to cost us."

So the couple walked up to the house and knocked on the door. A warm voice said, "Come on in." When they opened the door they saw the damage that was done: glass was all over the place, and a broken antique bottle was lying on its side near the broken window.

A man reclining on the couch asked, "Are you the people that broke my window?"

"Uh, yeah, sir. We're sure sorry about that," the husband replied.

"Oh, no apology is necessary. Actually I want to thank you... You see, I'm a genie and I've been trapped in that bottle for a thousand years. Now that you've released me, I'm allowed to grant three wishes. I'll give you each one wish, but if you don't mind, I'll keep the last one for myself."

"Wow, that's great!" the husband said. He pondered a moment and blurted out, "I'd like a million dollars a year for the rest of my life."

"No problem," said the genie. "You've got it. It's the least I can do. And I'll guarantee you a long, healthy life! And now you, young lady, what do you want?" the genie asked.

"I'd like to own a gorgeous home complete with servants in every country in the world."

"Consider it done," the genie said. "And your homes will always be safe from fire, burglary and natural disasters!"

"And now," the couple asked in unison, "what's your wish, genie?"

"Well, since I've been trapped in that bottle and haven't been with a woman in more than a thousand years, my wish is to have sex with your wife."

The husband looked at his wife and said, "Gee, honey, you know we both now have a fortune, and all those houses. What do you think?"

She mulled it over for a few moments and said, "You know, you're right. Considering our good fortune, I guess I wouldn't mind, but what about you, honey?"

"You know I love you, sweetheart," said the husband. "I'd do the same for you!"

So the genie and the woman went upstairs where they spent the rest of the afternoon enjoying each other in every way. After about three hours of non–stop sex, the genie rolled over and looked directly into her eyes and asked, "How old are you and your husband?"

"Why, we're both 35," she responded breathlessly.

"NO SHIT," he said. "Thirty–five and both of you still believe in genies?"

$$$$$

LESSON ONE

A man is getting into the shower just as his wife is finishing up her shower, when the doorbell rings. The wife quickly wraps herself in a towel and runs downstairs.

When she opens the door, there stands Bob, the next–door neighbor.

Before she says a word, Bob says, "I'll give you $800 to

drop that towel."

After thinking for a moment, the woman drops her towel and stands naked in front of Bob, after a few seconds, Bob hands her $800 and leaves.

The woman wraps back up in the towel and goes back upstairs.

When she gets to the bathroom, her husband asks, "Who was that?"

"It was Bob, the next door neighbor," she replies.

"Great," the husband says, "did he say anything about the $800 he owes me?"

MORAL OF THE STORY

If you share critical information pertaining to credit and risk with your shareholders in time, you may be in a position to prevent avoidable exposure.

LESSON TWO

A priest offered a nun a lift.

She got in and crossed her legs, forcing her gown to reveal a leg.

The priest nearly had an accident.

After controlling the car, he stealthily slid his hand up her leg.

The nun said, "Father, remember Psalm 129?"

The priest removed his hand. But, changing gears, he let his hand slide up her leg again.

The nun once again said, "Father, remember Psalm 129?"

The priest apologized, "Sorry sister but the flesh is weak."

Arriving at the convent, the nun sighed heavily and went on her way.

On his arrival at the church, the priest rushed to look up

Psalm 129. It said, "Go forth and seek, further up, you will find glory."

MORAL OF THE STORY

If you are not well informed in your job, you might miss a great opportunity.

LESSON THREE

A sales rep, an administration clerk, and the manager are walking to lunch when they find an antique oil lamp. They rub it and a genie comes out. The genie says, "I'll give each of you just one wish."

"Me first! Me first!" says the admin clerk. "I want to be in the Bahamas, driving a speedboat, without a care in the world."

Puff! She's gone.

"Me next! Me next! Says the sales rep. "I want to be in Hawaii, relaxing on the beach with my personal masseuse, an endless supply of Pina Coladas and the love of my life!"

Puff! He's gone.

"Okay, you're up," the genie says to the manager.

The manager says, "I want those two back in the office after lunch."

MORAL OF THE STORY

Always let your boss have the first say.

LESSON FOUR

An eagle was sitting on a tree resting, doing nothing. A small rabbit saw the eagle and asked him, "Can I also sit like you and do nothing?"

The eagle answered: "Sure, why not?"

So, the rabbit sat on the ground below the eagle and rested. All of a sudden a fox appeared, jumped on the rabbit and ate it.

MORAL OF THE STORY
To be sitting and doing nothing, you must be sitting vey very high up.

LESSON FIVE
A turkey was chatting with a bull. "I would love to able to get to the top of that tree," sighed the turkey, "but I haven't got the energy."
"Well, why don't you nibble on some of my droppings?" replied the bull. "They're packed with nutrients."
The turkey pecked at a lump of dung, and found it actually gave him enough strength to reach the lowest branch of the tree. The next day, after eating some more dung, he reached the second branch. Finally after a fourth night, the turkey was proudly perched at the top of the tree.
He was promptly spotted by a farmer, who shot him out of the tree.

MORAL OF THE STORY
Bull Shit might get you to the top, but it won't keep you there.

LESSON SIX
A little bird was flying south for the winter. It was so cold the bird froze and fell to the ground into a large field. While he was lying there— a cow came by and dropped some dung on him. As the frozen bird lay there in the pile of cow dung, he began to realize how warm he was.
The dung was actually thawing him out! He lay there all warm and happy, and soon began to sing for joy.
A passing cat heard the bird singing and came to investigate. Following the sound, the cat discovered the bird under the pile of cow dung, and promptly dug him out and ate him.

MORALS OF THE STORY

1. Not everyone who shits on you is your enemy.
2. Not everyone who gets you out of shit is your friend.
3. And when you're in deep shit, it's best to keep your mouth shut!

THUS ENDS THE FIVE MINUTE MANAGEMENT COURSE

$$$$$

Cake or bed

A husband is at home watching a football game when his wife interrupts, "Honey, could you fix the light in the hallway? It's been flickering for weeks now." He looks at her and says angrily, "Fix the lights now? Does it look like I have G.E. written on my forehead? I don't think so."

"Fine," then the wife asks, "Well then, could you fix the fridge door? It won't close right... "To which he replied, "Fix the fridge door? Does it look like I have Westinghouse written on my forehead? I don't think so."

"Fine," she says, "could you at least fix the steps to the front door? They are about to break." "I'm not a carpenter and I don't want to fix steps." He says, "Does it look like I have Ace Hardware written on my forehead? I don't think so. I've had enough of you, I'm going to the bar!!"

So he goes to the bar and drinks for a couple of hours... He starts to feel guilty about how he treated his wife, and decides to go home.

As he walks into the house he notices that the steps are already fixed. As he enters the house, he sees the hall light is working. As he goes to get a beer, he notices the fridge door is fixed.

"Honey," he asks, "How'd all this get fixed?" She said, "Well when you left I sat outside and cried. Just then a nice young man asked me what was wrong, and I told him. He offered to do all the repairs, and all I had to do was either go to bed with him or bake a cake." He said, "So what kind of cake did you bake?"

She replied, "Helloooooo. Do you see Betty Crocker written on my forehead?"

CHAPTER SIX

MANIFEST DESTINY

Nothing of value will ever go to those who don't work hard for their goals. And even then, for the guys who get blessings without toil, most of the time they'll squander the profits before they can ever accomplish anything of any value. Real talk!

If you really want to become a Pen Pal Pimp you're gonna have to make it happen yourself. You know, I lose pen pals all the time. Just the other day I checked my emails and my friend, Maria from Scotland sent me a message telling me that she's tryin to work things out with her ex–husband, etc... and she hoped I wouldn't be mad at her. I sent her a reply immediately, letting her know that I could never be mad at her. I let her know that I'm actually happy that she's able to rekindle the flame with her baby daddy, and that I hope nothing but positive energy comes her way. I ended the letter with a promise that I'll be here for her with open arms when she decides to come back home.

You know why I wasn't angry with her? Why I can't be mad at any pen pal for leaving me? Because I know that I'll find another one to take their place whenever I want one. I know it'll happen because I see it happening in my mind. Since I already see the outcome, my mind is subconsciously wired to make the moves that it takes to manifest my goals.

Everything I do when it comes to finding new pen pals happens automatically. I send out for every free prison publication there is, so I'm constantly finding names of people and organizations that write inmates. When I watch TV I make it work for me. How? When I have the channel on shows like Judge Judy I'll jot down the names of the Plaintiffs and Defendants along with the city and state they're from (yes, all that info is put in writing at the bottom of the screen when they enter the courtroom), so that I can later send it to my pen pal in Arizona so she can google their addresses for me. When I get stamps in the mail, instead of going to the poker table with them, I use them to pay for updates on my WriteAPrisoner.com profile. I do these things now without even thinking about it.

I call this manifesting my destiny. And you can do it too! All you have to do is start meditating on it. Visualize yourself being the MAN. Visualize yourself accomplishing all of your goals, and they will come true! Here's what you do:

1. Find a quiet spot during a quiet time of the day or night. Whether it's on your bunk in your cell, during count time, or during a solo stroll around the track. You need to find a place where you can be alone with your thoughts.

2. Slow your breathing down and push all other thoughts out of your mind. Concentrate on the mission at hand by telling yourself that right now is your manifestation time.

3. Once you've entered the realm of your mental that is clear to build in, start visualizing what it is that you want. You want mail, so see yourself getting mail. You want visits, phone calls, money; see it all. Visualize your life with all of that. Utilize this hunger in your chest that comes from that energy, feel it and own it because this will be the fuel that drives you to make it all happen.

4. Now, after you've established what you want, it's time

to see yourself putting in the work that it takes to achieve those things. Picture yourself writing letters; keeping files on all of your pen pals; imagine your pen pals reading your letters and writing you back. Do all of this as vividly as possible.

5. You have to repeat these steps as often as you can so that the whole process can become second nature to you. Second nature, like brushing your teeth in the morning, or tying your shoelaces... None of these things you have visualized should seem like work to you. It should be just part of your daily habits.

You are your own Lord and Master. You can accomplish anything you put your mind to, no matter what anyone else says, or how hard it may seem. It's all in your hands to mold and create the reality that you choose in life.

CHAPTER SEVEN

DECODED

I can't stand "inmates" who think K9's know the answer to every question in the world just because they wear a badge. Have you ever been in a debate with your celly, or someone else on the tier, and when the sound of keys jingling is heard, he'll say something like "Let's just ask officer Deepthroat..." These types act as if that badge makes the owner an oracle when in all actuality them folks are just normal people... normal people just like you and I.

So far, throughout this book I've been trying to censor myself because I know it's going to be sent into interior ciphers, and may be scrutinized by draconian mail room regulators. The above paragraph alone may get this book placed on some "censor lists" (sorry, Fla and TX DOC's). Nevertheless, I had to open up like that to wake a few of you up. My point is that people are people. Just because a person has a job working for the Dept. of Corrections it doesn't make them exceptionally smarter, wiser or holier than thou.

A woman is a woman whether she's a nurse, a parole agent or kitchen staff. Too many convicts forget this because of the line that has been drawn between us and them. I'm here to let you know that that line is imaginary. It doesn't exist. Any female can be cracked, regardless of her profession, as long as you got the right game.

And that's what this book is all about— giving you the game to enter the mental of any female you choose to court while you are in prison. Once you overcome the mental barrier that keeps you from approaching certain women, then you can move on. The next step is understanding that even though woman don't change—YOUR situation has. You are no longer on the street, so where you once could cash in on your rep, your looks, or your financial status— all those tools have gone out the window.

Something you have to keep in mind about being in an environment with thousands of men and only a hand full of women is that they're always gonna be someone who looks better than you, has more money than you and/or has more access to the females (better job, goes to trade or school). If you're serious about your mission you're really gonna have to be a MAC (Master at Communicating). You need to study your prey because it's literally impossible to use a "one–size–fits–all" method and have it work on all the females in this environment. You're gonna have to get to know them as individuals and learn their motivations. They all have them.

You certainly can have some success treating all women the same, but you'll always have blind spots, and this means you'll miss out on some opportunities. Where we're at, our chances of interacting with women are extremely limited, so if you miss one cue it might be the only chance you'll have in a long time. By tailoring your game to different types of women, and having a flexible approach, you'll be in a position to maximize your efforts.

Knowledge this: since women have been forced to adopt different survival techniques than us, the innate needs they have can't be understood by us unless it's drawn out and explained. This is the source of so many confusions because not only are men not aware of women's inner subconscious needs, females don't realize that we don't know them, and they naturally assume we do! This phenomenon tends to make relationships extremely complicated even though it doesn't have to be.

Women have three major psychological conflicts that they deal with. These conflicts are so intense that it forces them to adopt a dominant strategy to deal with them, and this strategy tends to become a part of their personality. How they deal with these conflicts dictates what turns them on and determines who they are attracted to. These three conflicts are Time, Sex, and Relationships.

TIME

Remember, along with a survival instinct, humans have evolved over hundreds of thousands of years to be a certain way. There are anomalies in any aspect of life, especially when dealing with people, but for the most part, other than cultural differences, biological needs are consistent. And one of those consistencies are that most people want to procreate another human in their image. The difference between men and women is that females have time constraints and we don't. After menopause, women can't conceive life, and they know this so it becomes a factor that they have to deal with daily.

Ultimately, this is where the term Cougars comes from. This is why you'll meet so many older women who are aggressive in their seduction tactics of younger men. They are driven by an internal desire to beat that clock....

SEX

In this chauvinistic world we live in, societies' rules dictate different freedoms for the different sexes. Where a man who has multiple sex partners is considered a stud, a woman who does the same is a slut. Let's take J–Lo for instance. What is the difference between J–Lo going through life falling in and out of love with different men and say, someone like George

Clooney? Nothing, yet, we see Clooney as a respectable man who enjoys life. And J–Lo is called an industry slut for doing the same thing.

Most of us (guys) have been in a make–out session where we're in it deep, kissing, rubbing, dry–humping and groping... Dick hard than a mothafucka! Then, out of nowhere, baby starts to pump the breaks. We call it being a "tease," but it's not always a game to them. Just think about it... the world puts a guilt trip on promiscuous women and some females take that shit to heart. This is the precise reason why sex becomes a
source of conflict for them.

RELATIONSHIP

How many of y'all have been raised by a single mother? Chances are, most of you who are reading this book have. Or, some of you have left single mothers out there. So I shouldn't have to go into how hard it is for women today. Not only do they have this innate, prewired urge to nurture their children, but they also have to juggle a career in the midst of all that.

In case you don't know it, there is a certain amount of pressure put on women by themselves and others for them to start a family. There are certain families that'll make them feel guilty for not getting married and having kids. And this can become an issue when they'd rather dedicate their lives to a career. All this has to be taken into consideration while we're operating on our seduction. Especially since, by asking them to fuck with you, you are essentially asking her to risk all that.

$$$$$

Okay, so now you know the 3 main conflicts all women have to deal with. Having the knowledge of these conflicts already puts you beyond the scope of the average man. That's cool, but it's not enough. Let's keep going...

Yes, all females have to deal with these same basic problems, but not all women are the same. What separates them are the ways they adapt to deal with these problems. It's like there's an internal war going on in their minds and there are two ways of dealing with it. You need to pay attention because the routes they take are opposite of one another and you have to be able to recognize the differences if you plan on capitalizing off the openings they offer.

Of course I'm gonna give you the game to overcome each line of defense, but you have to understand them before you can manipulate them. What I'm gonna do now is break down their defenses, but don't take it for granted because it'll get a lot deeper as we go. So, right now I'm gonna use certain terms that I'll continue to use throughout the rest of this book. They are: RENTER/BUYER, LIAR/OWNER, SHREWD/DREAMER. You're gonna have to become familiar with these terms if you want to understand the rest of this book.

SO PAY ATTENTION!!!

TIME

It's like this... in most prisons the inmates have a representative who meets with the staff to discuss certain program issues. In Cali we call them MAC Reps (Men's Advisory Council Representative). Every race has at least one MAC Rep. They are the liaison between the inmates and police, so it's vital that you choose one who isn't meek and can do the job right.

Let's say your current MAC Rep is about to go home in 3 months. You got this time limit to pick and choose another (competent) MAC Rep. There are two ways to do this:

1. You can pick 3 different guys and watch them for a certain amount of time, then choose the best one for the job.

2. You can pick the first person who volunteers for the job and you can train him.

Neither one of these options are the perfect remedy, but they'll work. These are the tactics that women use to choose the best man. They either date or court several men at once, or they'll latch on to one at a time and try to mold him ("fix him") into the ideal man.

From now on, I'll refer to the women who date/court multiple guys at once as "RENTERS." And I'll refer to the women who try to fix men as "BUYERS."

Remember: RENTERS and BUYERS!

SEX

We've covered the fact that society has different rules for men as women especially when it comes to sex. But here's the thing: Regardless of how they act, most woman love sex. It feels good and the intimacy of it gives females a specific connection that they all long for. The problem comes from the judgement that comes along with it.

I grew up in the crack era. From a young age me and most of my friends used to post up on the block with pockets full of rocks. Along with that came a certain lifestyle and one aspect of that life was the female crackheads who would come along wanting to get a hit without having any money to pay for it.

Where I'm from it was frowned upon to trick your rocks off to get your rocks off. The homies would laugh you off the block if you got caught trickin' with a dope fiend. And since the fiends knew this, if you ever made 'em mad the first thing they'd do is run their mouth about what you did with them, or how they saw you getting suck'd up by one of your homeboy's aunties in the back of an abandoned house.

When this used to happen there were two ways to handle it:

1. You lied about it. Say it never happened.
2. Own it! Ride it out like a champ. I mean, how can you lose? You're the guy who got his dick sucked.

That's exactly how women deal with the sex conflict. They'll either act like they don't like it; that it doesn't mean as much to them as it does to guys. Or, they'll own it. They play it off like it's not a big deal.

"Liars" will pretend sex or sexual thoughts don't happen, they'll repress their ideas about sex, making it harder for guys to have sex with them. "Owners" see sex as insignificant, and let it happen all the time.

Remember: LIARS and OWNERS!

TIME

We all know that women are biologically wired to remain conscious about the options to breed. On average, they have about a 25 year window to have babies and raise a family. The problem is that those years are the same years that people use to go to school and build a career. It doesn't help that both of those things take up so much time that it leaves them with barely enough time to do both.

In this setting, you're gonna run into two different kinds of women. There are some who will be leery of stepping into a relationship with you because they're afraid of losing their job. They see their job as a career that they've worked their whole lives for. It's their livelihood.

Then there's the ones who can see themselves with you

after you get out of prison. They may be willing to quit their job in hopes of starting a life with you.

The first example is what I'll call a "SHREWD." She's very serious, sees the world in black and white and very seldom deviates from her set course. The second example I'll refer to as a "DREAMER." To her, the world is full of possibilities, she's very optimistic.

SHREWDS focus on their careers almost to the point of eliminating the dating aspect of their life. DREAMERS sometimes don't even consider their careers when love is in question.

Remember: SHREWDS and DREAMERS!

Understanding these 3 dimensions of women is critical to MAC'n. If you can understand the thinking that is taking place in the minds of women regarding the conflicts of Time, Sex and Relationships you will be a beast at communicating with the opposite sex.

Even if you don't realize it yet, I just gave you a lot of game to take in. I recommend that you go back and reread this chapter before you move on, because if you don't understand the definitions or differences between RENTERS/BUYERS; LIARS/OWNERS; SHREWDS/DREAMERS, you're gonna get lost in translation throughout the next few chapters.

CHAPTER EIGHT

THE PLAYGIRL

Personality profile: Renter/Liar/Dreamer

The Playgirl is like that sexy librarian we've all fantasized about. If you're not on your shit she'll slide right past you because she's quiet and good at camouflaging herself. She's an observer. She doesn't wear her emotions on her sleeve and she tends to keep her personal life under wraps.

It's like she has these walls around her, they're really not that high, but there is barbed wire across the top, making it just that much harder to penetrate. All you gotta do is walk up to it and look in and you'll see that she's really sweet, sexy and exciting. Baby has a lot to offer, but that's what makes her vulnerable and she knows it. Before she ever lets you in you're gonna have to show her that you won't smother or pressure her. Nevertheless, romance and intimacy is what she longs for.

Playgirls are usually in their early to mid–20's , The main obstacle separating you from your ultimate goal will be separating yourself from the competition. She isn't shy so she'll talk to you, but you can't get stuck in the "Basic–Zone" or "Friend–Zone." The only way to do this is by intriguing her. Being different, yet fulfilling her desires. Let your body language telegraph your intentions, but never act clingy.

Keep in mind that one of the Playgirl's psychological characteristics is a Dreamer! This is why her ideal man is unrealistic, and shit makes it hard for her to choose her Mr. Right. This is especially complicated since you'll be stepping to her while you're in prison. B.U.T., real talk: What a woman fantasizes about, and what she responds to in real time, are two different things.

She responds to a man who doesn't need her more than she needs him. All the men in her life are chasing her; they are one of her options. You have the most leverage with her if she perceives herself to be one of your options. So she must want you more than you want her, and you must convey that you're dating other women. But how do you make her interested in you in the first place, when she has a gang of other cats surrounding her?

The answer is in the Dreamer aspect of her psychological profile. You need to literally sweep her off her feet. Now we have all heard that saying before, and it means different things to different women. However, in the Playgirl's case, you gotta play the classic man. She wants a man who'll arouse her, seduce her, take her down and tame her.

If you play this role to the "T" she'll melt. She'll be loyal, lustful and passionate. She'll go so hard in the paint that you won't even need another female in your life. This is why so many guys go after Playgirls. It's not easy to climb that wall, though. But once you get over it you've hit the jackpot!

HER TECHNIQUES

Playgirls are just like MACs. They're RENTERS, don't ever forget it. They'll keep 3 or 4 dudes on their call list. The thing is, you need to over–stand the reason she does this is because her ideal man is unrealistic, so she has to have several different guys to fulfill each one of her needs. If she was a BUYER she'd lock on to one guy, but she's not. Remember this and you'll stay one step ahead of the competition.

When I was breaking down the category of LIARS. I basically kept it along the lines of sex. Yes. They'll deny their urges, or fantasies, but they got 'em. Don't forget it. That's why she's harder to get than OWNERS. This doesn't mean it's impossible to penetrate her mental, it just means you gotta work harder to climb over the barriers.

Here's the thing: As a DREAMER, the Playgirl has it in the back of her mind that she will one day meet her King. In a sense, she's always looking for her King by being passive and leaving a social vacuum for men to take the lead. The irony is, her coolness makes most men uneasy and lacking confidence. She won't tell you what to do… she'll just sit back and observe what kind of person you are.

POINTS OF CONQUEST

Mouth Piece.

If you step to a Playgirl with some game–goofy shit, one of two things are gonna happen:

1.She'll ignore you completely.
2.She'll sit there and look at you like you're an idiot.

Based on the fact that she's a RENTER, you're not gonna stimulate her mental by trying to get at her on a deeper level. The best approach, conversationally is to start talking about something that's happening right then and there. Come on, you're in prison, someone's always doing some funny shit. As long as you're not dry–snitching, speak on it.

Another surefire way to get at a LIAR/RENTER is to tease her. Even though she acts like she's not sexual— she is!

It's what's on her mind. The thing is she's in denial about it, so you gotta keep it light. Be playful. This doesn't mean you should tell her she's fat or ugly— that's not teasing, that's abuse. But if she ever tries to be "cool," laugh and tell her she's cute.

Playgirls keep a cipher of men getting at them, so you gotta set yourself apart from them. Even if you can't stop thinking about fucking the shit out of her asshole, don't let her see that side of you. Everyone else is already doing that. If you really want her to fall for you, you need to appear unpredictable as well as uninterested sexually.

And all this has to be done while you're staying out of the "Basic–Zone." Once you enter that category you're lost in it forever…

CLOSING THE DEAL

It's actually kinda easy to close the deal with Playgirls, simply because other cats are basic and don't have a mouth–piece. The main thing you need to remember is not to try to sweet–talk her and don't try to get sexual either. Yet, at the same time, you don't wanna ask her the same questions the next cat is asking. Keep it light and keep it fun. Talk about funny shit that's happening around you.

You know what, just get her to do all the talking. She's the quiet one, which means, once you get her talking she won't shut up. And that's a good thing because her Dreamer nature will eventually take over, and her fantasies about you will do the rest.

If you're trying to get her to do all the talking— you gotta ask some good questions. Ask her what is about her job that she likes (if she likes it). Ask her what she'd like to do if she wasn't doing what she's doing. The best questions are "why did you do/think/say/that?" and "how did that make you feel?"

CHAPTER NINE
COCAINE

Personality profile: Renter/Owner/Dreamer

We all know them fast girls that live like there's no tomorrow. Some people call them "Rippers," some people call them "Party–Girls." I'ma call 'em "Cocaine." They're turnt up and always leave you wanting more. Cocaine is a mixture of Renter, Owner and Dreamer. Everything about her is loose and fun, the thing is, her energy is contagious so every other man in her cipher is gonna be feeling everything that you're feeling about her. What these interprets to is that you're gonna have a gang of competition, and the only way you'll be able to pull her is if you know what you're doing.

Whenever you're working on a Renter there will always be competition. So you're already in a situation where you will have to quickly separate yourself from others. With Cocaine, you gotta be aggressive. Yeah, be at her, but don't ever make her feel like you're just trying to get sexual gratification. That part of the game will come with her, but you can't make her feel like that's all you're after.

HER CRAVINGS

Cocaine has such a strong urge to pull the "unattainable" guy that she often picks the wrong guy. Some dudes (especially "inmates") don't think it's possible to crack a female in prison. So, when the opportunities arise they don't even see it! B.U.T. Cocaine might take "blindness" for "interesting." What you have to do is recognize this, and utilize the right technique to crack her.

The biggest challenge men face with Cocaine is that she likes to be the chaser. She wants to be the one who chooses, and chases, the man. The irony is that she ends up chasing the guy that either, a) doesn't want her, or b) wasn't the "strong silent type" but was actually an insecure, immature guy that simply didn't know what to say.

This woman is impulsive. But nonetheless, she is a woman and has feminine drives to contribute and nurture. As long as you have a strong vision and are self–controlled she'll always be drawn to you.

HER TECHNIQUES

Cocaine will fuck with a guy just because he's hot. Nevertheless, "hot" can mean many different things to her: well–dressed, well–kept, confident, nice smile, alpha male, nice abs, etc. This girl gets different things from different men, and loves the newness of the stimuli. She likes to try different men for their kissing styles, dick sizes, fashion and music styles; the list is endless.

The one thing she doesn't like is the overly romantic type. Cocaine doesn't want to read love letters or poems. She doesn't want to fantasize about walking hand in hand on the beach... she's all about the here and now.

You gotta strive to be the guy she chases and is almost out of her reach.

As an Owner, she's most likely seen and done it all. If

you are gonna put sex in the mix (kissing, rubbing, pulling your dick out) you gotta be bold. You gotta be unique and sure of yourself. If not, you risk putting yourself in the "basic" category.

Cocaine is usually young and not worried about her future. It's all about NOW! You Only Live Once... YOLO! This is great for a convict because this is the one who'll bring you phones and work. She's the one you can make thousands with. The thing is, she gets bored fast. If you crack Cocaine you gotta keep her interested or she'll move on to the next guy.

POINTS OF CONQUEST

Mouthpiece

You can step to Cocaine any way you want. The catch is you have to be totally sure of yourself. You must also keep it light and fun and always be bold. Don't try to game her, and don't forget that she's an Owner so sex ain't new or special to her. Any sign of timidity is a major turn off for her.

Here's some tips for getting Cocaine's attention:
1. Be loud
2. Stand tall, and position yourself in her personal space
3. Smile and look her in the eye when YOU are talking

It's not hard to get Cocaine's attention. It's keeping it that's the challenge. Your best bet is to find out what her interests are. It may sound obvious, but most guys screw this up by asking interview–style questions. Pay attention to her— she wears her life on her sleeve. She likely will wear, talk about, or do something that is interesting to her. Comment on it and relate to it.

She's also a Renter, so tease her immediately. Even more

than Playgirls, Cocaine responds very powerfully to being teased. Just make sure you can take what you can dish out this woman loves to banter. Stay on your toes and stay focused on lightly pointing her silly quirks and mistakes. But, always back it up with warmth.

I also gotta say something that any real MAC knows as Common sense. Still... I'm gonna say it cuz some of you cat's be on some other shit! Cocaine is going to fuck with other guys. That's what she does, she's a Renter/Owner/Dreamer. All of these attributes describe a social being. So don't get mad when you hit a corner and you see her laughing at the next man's jokes. Just be patient because she will make her way back to you. And when she does, fuck what she was going through with the last guy, start off right where you left off!

CLOSING THE DEAL

It may seem counter–intuitive, but with a Renter, especially a Renter/Owner, finding one deep topic and building on it can have a profound effect. But keep it as a contrast, an exemption to the rule; keep the conversation light, positive and rhythmic.

Renters usually have something they're passionate about. If you can find out what that is— lock onto and build with her about it. This is what'll separate you from the others.

Cocaine is in a class of her own. When she chases you it won't be like she's trying to be next to you during her whole shift. It won't be like she'll spend more time with you than with other people. No, it'll come out in the quality of conversations you'll have with her. She'll talk to you about things that she doesn't talk about with other prisoners. And, in return you pay her back with attention and sexual gratification. See... there's a time for everything.

CHAPTER TEN

ROMANTIC VISIONARY

Personality profile: Owner/Liar/Dreamer

For the Romantic Visionary, daydreaming about the perfect man is an old and favorite pastime. The potential of long–term relationships are the foundation of all of her goals and dreams.

One of her major turn–offs is the loss of trust. If you're in a relationship with another woman when you first meet a Romantic Visionary, the worst move you can make is to lie about it. This is one of the female types who demand honesty. If she feels you can't be trusted— all her hopes of cultivating a relationship are destroyed.

HER CRAVINGS

If you ask a Romantic Visionary what kind of man she's attracted to, she'll most likely use words like patient, gentle and sweet. Yet, nine times outta ten she'll end up with a thug or "bad–boy" type. This is because what she's really looking for is emotional strength.

What she really needs (wants) is a ying to her yang. Since she is so sensitive and sentimental she needs a sort of counterbalance. If you plan on building a relationship with this type you have to understand her moods, and be willing to comfort her when the time calls for it.

The Romantic Visionary wants a man to save. She is attracted to the mysterious, unattainable, unreachable, angry, depressed, artistic and out of bounds. This means YOU! She wants to bring a hard man in from the cold. She wants to warm his heart with her love. But you must never forget: It's the challenge itself that is attractive. Once you turn soft you'll lose her.

HER TECHNIQUES

The Romantic Visionary is a Buyer, so she looks for sexual gratification and emotional fulfillment from one man, not several. When she meets a guy who catches her interest, she immediately begins to size him up as a long–term partner.

If she gets the indication that he doesn't have the capacity to bond with her, she will move on. But here's where it gets tricky. A man who is moody, or wild, or living on the edge actually indicates the potential for rapport because he is emotional, AND he's not trying to pursue her.

Her conflicts come from her urge to want to save, nurture and take care of people she cares about, but at the same time, dealing with society's status quo of getting money and providing for herself financially. This'll both work for you and against you because she'll be willing to help you out with money, yet she'll shy away from breaking the law.

And once you do get her to start breaking you off, you gotta make sure you don't start looking needy, or weak cuz she'll lose attraction. The goal is always longevity. The Romantic Visionary is looking for someone who's loose yet strong. The second you turn submissive she'll start looking elsewhere...

POINTS OF CONQUEST

Mouthpiece

When you're chasing a Buyer it pays to be straight–forward. Why? Because she either has a man at home, or she's looking for one. And if she has a man out there, chances are he's lacking in one or two of the areas (sexual/emotional) she's looking for in a man. The best thing for you is if her current man isn't measuring up to her emotional needs. That's where you'll really be able to excel.

"Straight–forward" doesn't always mean telling her explicitly that you're attracted to her. It can be conveyed through the eyes and body. Eye contact creates sexual tension without the need for any specific wordplay, but takes a lot of calibration. A good rule of thumb is to act like her eyes and your eyes are magnets— hold eye contact a beat longer than normal, but don't try to stare her down.

With a Romantic Visionary you have to take control of the gears. She'll let you dictate the speed of your relationship. If you shut down, she'll shut down. If you turn up, she'll turn up. Use that to your advantage!

Create a dynamic of "you and her vs. the world" as soon as possible. This is easier than it sounds— find common ground, and then make a joke about the rest of the world/people being different.

Whenever you're around her, keep your energy smooth and dominant. Don't let it seem like you stress too much. In other words, be an optimist, but give out the aura of a man who will stand tall under pressure.

CLOSING THE DEAL

Now, the Romantic Visionary is the one you want to fantasize with. Since she's a Buyer she thinks long term. Based on she's a Dreamer, romance and fantasy are ingrained in her thinking process. And as a Liar, she tries to act like she doesn't think about sex but it does mean a lot to her. So, basically, this is the one that you want to sell the dreams of "life–after–prison."

You can tell her things like you're taking (or want to take) college courses, or a trade so that you can provide for her once you get out of prison. Whatever topic you discuss with her, always use the terms "us" and "we."

Another route that works with her is to play on her romantic tendencies. Give her a SOB story about how you've had your heart broken in the past. Let her know that you don't have time to fuck with "girls," that you need a "woman" because you're not about to let your heart get broken again.

Remember: The Romantic Visionary is always sizing you up for "life–after–prison."

So pay attention to your body language. Relax your body and face. Respect her personal space and use eye contact to show her that you are focused on her. She's studying your energy to gauge her future with you.

CHAPTER ELEVEN

BONNIE (and CLYDE)

Personality profile: Buyer/Owner/Dreamer

Nine times outta ten, Bonnie is beautiful, stylish and far from square. She keeps her hair and nails done, dresses in clothes that fit right. She does this because she's searching for a man (Clyde) and wants to be ready at all times.

The catch is, she looks so good that you'll automatically assume she has a man, so most guys don't even approach her on that level. But Bonnie is often the victim of repeated heartbreak because she wears her heart on her sleeve and lives in a world of hopes and ideals. She is very passionate and heats up fast. Often this passion gets her into trouble, because she is prone to sweet talk and will let her emotions cloud her need to sort and pick the best man for the long run.

If you can prove to her that you're in it for the long run, half your work will already be done. Since she's an Owner, sexual energy flows from her being. If you can turn her on in that department, then chances are, the other half of your job will be fulfilled and you can kick your feet up. Just know that Bonnie needs passion and a hope for the future.

HER CRAVINGS

Bonnie is looking for a mixture of strength and sensitivity. She doesn't care about the Alpha Male. She wants a man who is mature, yet sensitive. She won't look at you like you're weak if you talk about your hopes, dreams, fears, or past experiences that went wrong. She needs to know that you have potential to overcome your vulnerabilities.

As a Buyer, she's the type that'll lock into one guy and invest all her energy into him. This doesn't mean she won't react positively towards sexual innuendos, or activities— just as long as you add a vibe that says there's potential for a relationship. Which shouldn't be hard in your predicament.

HER TECHNIQUES

Her techniques for finding a man are fluid. It all depends on how she's feeling. She might go on a clubbin' binge for a few weeks, or she might look for one at work. Sometimes she won't even have a man, but you'll never be able to tell by just looking at her.

Bonnie is both, "old school" and "new school" with her views on gender roles. Old school in the fashion that she respects the man. She wants a man to take care of her and lead her. But, what I mean by "new school" is when it comes to sexual stimulation, she's far form a nun. She'll hold a full on convo with you while you're in the shower, yet again, she'll only be this open with you if she likes you.

Since she's a Dreamer her ultimate goal is to one day be a homemaker. What this means is that her job, although necessary, doesn't actually mean as much to her as her need to find the right man. This is great for the right convict, trust me; I know!

POINTS OF CONQVEST

Mouthpiece

Personally, I like Bonnies cuz I'ma Clyde! The best way to get at her is straight forward. Be honest and direct. Tell her that you like her, but she's so fine that you always forget what you're gonna say when you finally get in her face. She's not gonna react to cockiness or aggressiveness. It's like you gotta be hard— yet seem to fumble a lil…

You can hit Bonnie with a one–liner, but you gotta make her feel like she's unique. Like she's the only one your eyes are interested in.

Immediately after breaking the ice, ask her questions about her life, and relate with your own experiences. Keep a nice balance of give and take, and keep your focus on how she thinks and feels about the topic. Don't get caught in logical facts— her Dreamer side gets bored with that. Focus on what makes her tick and show her what makes you tick. This appeals to her Buyer strategy of finding a guy that wants to get to know her over the long–run.

CLOSING THE DEAL

This woman gets turned on by talking about sex, and loves a man who can match her in passion. She embraces a guy who knows how to turn her on mentally, before she gets physical. To really engage this woman, you must incorporate an element of sexuality in your conversation. Obviously it's good to do this within a couple minutes.

Strong eye contact is important, but don't invade her personal space initially. When you get the sense that she is interested, close the space and create a bubble around the two of you with your focus.

CHAPTER TWELVE

SECRET LOVER

Personality profile: Renter/Liar /Shrewd

Just like the other Renter–Liar type, the Secret Lover has two sides to her personality. There's the mysterious–yet–innocent exterior. And there's the passionate and sensitive woman inside. Only a select few get to see this hidden part of her.

The Secret Lover is a giver by nature. She wants to be the source of her man's happiness. But this can open her up to being taken advantage of so she's very selective when choosing what man to bestow her blessings on.

What I just described can also be considered a Buyer instead of a Renter. And, in a big way, she IS a Buyer. The thing is she knows her faults and this is what makes her a Renter. Because she knows her tendency to take care of people is so strong, as a defense mechanism she keeps several different projects in play to protect her from investing too much time and energy on the wrong guy.

If you ever reach the level where you get sexual with the Secret Lover, she's gonna be one of the best fucks you've ever had. She will do the things she does to please you because that is what pleases her. And this will show in other categories as well. This is the type of woman who will bring you food from the streets and put money on your books. So you'll be flooded in hygiene and food, she'll make sure your locker stays fat. Be sure of that.

The Secret Lover knows how to hide her emotions. She's not gonna light up every time she sees you. If you're not aware of this phenomenon it may throw you off like it does with most of the other guys. But don't let it throw you off her scent. You have to do YOU because this is what she'll expect. If you half–step she'll get turned off and you'll lose her.

HER CRAVINGS

As a Renter, this woman is uncomfortable with too much intensity and romance at first. She would prefer to keep the conversation on situational topics rather than getting too personal. She also needs a guy who is persistent but not too sexual or aggressive. Sexual tension makes her uneasy as she represses that side of herself throughout the day. Again this is a self–protective mechanism— there's definitely a wild side to this
woman.

The Secret Lover is extremely horny, but doesn't show it. She doesn't even see herself as a sexual person; in the privacy of a broom closet she'll let loose in ways you can only imagine. But you better not try to get her to talk about sex in front of others. Nevertheless, always keep in mind that in her mind she's always in sex mode. Trust that if she sees you in the shower — her pussy'll get wet!

HER TECHNIQUES

The Secret Lover will fraternize with other men because she can relate to the masculine way of thinking. She hates drama and thinks most women are catty. This is why she meets a lot of men, and has a lot of guys chasing her. There is something about her mysterious personality that draws men in.

Listen: Do not try to talk about sex with the Secret Lover. It's gonna turn her off because she doesn't see herself like that. Secret Lovers think about sex so much that when the right guy comes along— she'll blow his mind. But till then, it's her lil' secret, and that is how she wants to keep it.

The Shrewd in her keeps her career–orientated. What this means to you is she's not likely to bring you anything illegal. And you're not gonna be able to entice her with the promise of riches because she wants to be the one who does the nurturing. So, not only is she not gonna risk her job to bring you anything, she's not enticed by money because she wants to be the breadwinner. If you can wrap your mind around that, you'll be extremely successful with a Secret Lover.

POINTS OF CONQUEST

Mouthpiece

The best way to approach a Renter, as mentioned earlier, is to make a comment on something in the environment. If you give her a compliment, make sure it's something unrelated to her body. Whereas you can tell a Buyer you love how her dress fits around her curves, a Renter would be very uncomfortable hearing this. Especially a R/L/S— she doesn't see herself as a sexual person in general— only with that one special guy.

Non–sexual compliments are fine, however. If she just got her hair done for example, just tell her "I like your hair."

Where a Dreamer reacts to being teased, the Shrewd doesn't need that to be interested in you. If you can do something as a team, this will separate you from the other guys. Ideally, she's a boss in a kitchen, or some sort of outside service where you can work with her on a daily basis. Work hard at your job and this will automatically create an attraction.

The Secret Lover is cool with talking about anything. She is like one of your guy friends— any random topic is valid. Just don't get too psychological. Some women love to explore the way people think. To a Shrewd, concert subjects are more interesting— travel, work, school, sports, her dog, etc.

The main way to build momentum with the Secret Lover is to NOT say or do anything sexual. This helps her feel at ease. Most guys screw this up. She'll actually respect you more if you can treat her like a person first— a teammate and partner.

CLOSING THE DEAL

The Secret Lover responds powerfully to the "us" frame of mind. You have to create a team mentality in everything you do. Use words like we, we're, we'll, us, let's, ours... remember, there ain't no I in team. The ideal setting for this seduction is if she is your boss in a kitchen, building, or a laundry room. Also: Whenever you're on a mission to crack a female, you want to stay outta trouble. You have more opportunities to meet women when you're able to move around. This will help a lot when you're dealing with a Renter because she has so many different guys around her— you want to be that one that's been around the longest. Since people are always moving around in prison, the longer you're around, the more it'll seem like you two have been through a lot together. This feeds right into the frame of mind!

Let your body language ooze confidence. Be loud, stand up straight, and talk like you expect people to listen. When you ask her to do something, look her in the eyes. Don't be bossy— act like you are making the call for the sake of the "team."

CHAPTER THIRTEEN

FEMME FATALE

Personality profile: Renter/Owner/Shrewd

The Femme Fatale is a Renter, Owner, Shrewd. This combination makes her a very confident, sexual, independent woman. She is a Diva— not in the dramatic sense— but in the sense that she is strong, sexy and has a presence that intimidates a lot of men. That's good news for any guy reading this, as you can move forward confidently. Simply understanding her and knowing how to handle her is massively attractive, as she sees most men as weak and insecure. This is very frustrating to her, as she is very horny, but also very career focused. She doesn't have time to coddle egos. In a sense, her attitude screens out the weak.

If you can keep your cool, not get emotionally needy, she'll be the best you ever had. However, if you get upset when she's too busy to give you attention, or you seem nervous when speaking to her, she'll sense this and discard you like yesterday's trash. One thing she doesn't respect is a weak man.

Don't take this to mean she's cold–blooded. It's not that, it's that she is well tuned in with her wants and needs and she's not going to settle for less. She wants a real man, a strong man and a confident man.

Real, strong, and confident doesn't mean acting hard or arrogant. Being a man means "knowing your edge." Knowing who you are and not being afraid to admit your weaknesses conveys strength. Realizing when you really know something is confidence. And communicating with the Femme Fatale in an honest way will show her you're REAL!

HER CRAVINGS

The Femme Fatale is very sexual, her mind is always on it. Most the time she's not looking for anything else other than sex. If you were in the free–world she'd be the ideal side–chick because all she really wants is a friend to kill them guts every once in a while.

Baby is looking for a friend, a homeboy who respects her mind. She doesn't want someone who will be clingy. Remember, she's a Shrewd so her career means a lot to her. You'll fit right into her lane if you have your own career goals, because she doesn't want all of your time. Mutual respect for each other's goals is the foundation for a long term relationship.

She wants the ongoing experience of seducing you. She feels powerful when she can use her beauty, energy and skill to turn you on. She likes to perpetually chase, but not in a schoolgirl way. Seducing a man is how she gets her power fix. Throughout the week, she will need an ego boost, and will need to feel sexy. She gets high knowing that a man is hungry for her, not because he's HORNY, but because of something she did to excite him.

HER TECHNIQUES

Ms. Femme Fatale knows that working at a prison means she's surrounded by horny guys. Even her coworkers are chasing

MIKE ENEMIGO & KING GURU

her. Yes, she enjoys the attention, but she doesn't want the guys who are on her "nuts." She's looking for the one guy who is a challenge.

Listen: There's no need for games or any kind of deception with her. As long as you're not running around like a hyper, love–sick puppy who smells pussy— you'll be a contrast to all the suckas who are always catering to her. Once she sees the man in you, she'll chase you. Real talk!

The Femme Fatale may at some point want a family, but she knows that in this day and age, a women can't rely on men to support them. She believes in being independent and paying her own bills. She is likely not going to be satisfied staying home until after she's had kids. However, as with all women, she has the need to nurture her man in order to strengthen the bond. She does this by helping in practical ways. She can help you get a job after prison. She likely knows a lot of people and has a good amount of connections.

Let her help you, challenge her to seduce you, never lose your cool and respect her.

POINTS OF CONQUEST

Mouthpiece

Don't step to her with a bunch of flashy talk and one–liners. She doesn't react to the "ra–ra." She wants a confident man, a real man. And she's been bred to sniff one out on call.

This means you should be very down to earth and casual in your approach. She'll wonder why you aren't fawning over her like every other guy. My favorite way to approach this type of woman is to give her a genuine compliment, but in a way that says I'm used to beauty and it's not a big deal.

If you give her a compliment, you can't put too much on it. Remember, everyone else is telling her she's a super model.

If you tell her she's looking "alright today" she'll burn up inside because she's used to people telling her she looks beautiful every day. That'll trigger a chase and that is what you want!

It's easy to berner the interest of the Femme Fatale for two reasons. First, she loves to chase, to seduce— it's how she gets her power fix. Second, every other guy is groveling to get in her pants. So it's simply a matter of not doing that. She will naturally want to conquer you.

Talk openly about your goals, failures, interests and silly childhood memories, and your most recent embarrassing moment. And ask about hers as well. Keep the topic on passions, goals and the mistakes that make us human.

Patience is the key with this woman. This one might be hard if you're not used to this, but you have to pull your attention away at the right moments. Right when you think a "basic" cat would go in for the kill is the exact moment when you should pull away. This works especially well with her because she loves the chase.

CLOSING THE DEAL

The best topic to talk to a Femme Fatale about is sex. And this is your opportunity to shine. Since she is always thinking about it, it won't be hard to get her pussy wet.
The objective is to get her hot and bothered, but for you to stay cool, calm and collective. She's always sizing you up, so you have to play chess.

She's the type that will go out of her way to catch you pissing, or in the shower. She's not looking for the biggest dick in the world, but she does want to know that you are secure with your manhood.

She wants a man who is passionate. It's not fun to give pleasure to someone who is unresponsive. And it's not fun to think your lover is just going through the motions. She needs to know that once she turns you on, you will be an animal. Convey this by discussing sex, goals, and everything else, with enthusiasm.

Now, keep in mind that there is a difference between being passionate about women and being aroused by every woman. The Femme Fatale will talk to you about ass, tits and pussy, but if you don't follow those convo's up with some type of sign that you're interested in a passionate relationship it'll turn her off and she'll lose interest in you.

When you make eye contact with her, hold it for one extra beat than would be "platonic" or polite. Then look away. It's kind of like you're saying, within that one brief moment, "You want me."

Keep a calm, slightly mischievous look on your face, as if you know something no one else does, and you are holding back a secret smile. You aren't fooled by her swagger. You know she's a sexy beast and just dying to sink her fangs in you.

Don't get caught looking at her ass or tits. Boring, she thinks. She knows that good foreplay starts everywhere else. Let her catch you glancing at her neckline, her lips, her hair. Think about how much fun it'd be to grab a handful, she'll sense what you're thinking about by the look in your eyes.

CHAPTER FOURTEEN

THE SAGE

Personality Profile: Buyer/Liar/ Shrewd

One of the hardest females to crack is the Sage. She's extremely picky and cautious in her approach to dating. For most guys the time and effort it takes to seduce her is too overwhelming, yet the payoff for a convict totally outweighs all efforts. Especially since we have an abundance of time.

Like the other Liar/Shrewd, she is a giver. She sees her time with you as a gift that she can't just give away to anyone. But, in contrast to the Secret Lover, she is inclined to invest in her relationship with you. A Renter will hold back and protect her emotions. A Buyer will dive in and contribute heavily in the relationship, emotionally and otherwise.

This is perfect for you since your ultimate goal is total devotion. The Sage is in a real position to contribute to your life and both of you know this. The great part is that she wants to do what's right by you just as much as you want her to.

The only problem I can see with her is that once you establish a relationship with her she is likely to get extremely attached. It's common in both Buyer/Liar types. The good news is that her Shrewd side understands that getting too clingy can arouse suspicion and possibly cost her job. If you guys can keep this aspect of her personality under wraps then you'll win!

The Sage does not like to chase men. She wants to be swept off her feet, and once she is— the rest will be on her. She'll seduce herself.

HER CRAVINGS

Being in prison is actually a plus for you when it comes to seducing the sage. Her ideal man is one who needs her. She wants a man who she can help, nurture, and even save. It's absolutely essential that you let her know how much you appreciate what she does for you.

It can be easy to take advantage of this woman. What you gotta hope for is that she hasn't already tried a relationship with a convict who got out and dogged her out. If this has happened it'll make your job a lot harder.

Yet, all in all, as long as she can be the nurturing, helpful woman she wants to be, around you, and you appreciate her for it, she'll be okay with keeping things casual and open. But her main goal is to be your main chick, so don't let her know you got a baby–mamma at home.

HER TECHNIQUES

The Sage looks for long–term potential. Not a boyfriend, per se, but a guy who is interested in her as a person. She has a Shrewd perspective on men, so she knows that if she gives in too fast, she'll devalue herself in your eyes. This ruins the chances of her gaining your devotion.

Conversation itself is an investment, as is all the time she spends with you. She feels vulnerable. You must build her confidence so that she feels like she has some power, not like a helpless victim. If you can get her to initiate interactions, and do things to turn you on, she will begin to feel empowered. But don't forget that she sees the relationship through a Buyer's eyes. Everything she does, even if it's to seduce you, is an investment she can't take back.

Counteracting her emotional sensitivity is the fact that she has a career, works hard, and is likely financially independent. She doesn't look to men to support her. She can do that herself. She wants ONE MAN who appreciates her. At the same time, she understands that we are not in the 1950's anymore, and most relationships start out casual and light. Essentially this woman performs a balancing act between Buyer–Liar and Shrewd.

POINTS OF CONQUEST

Mouthpiece

The Sage wants to know that you chose her out of a crowd and was specifically interested in her! A direct, sincere compliment is a great way to open up a dialogue. However, if you say something too sexual it'll turn her off because she'll think you're a player. (She's a Liar, and most Liars have a cynical view of men's sexual intentions.)

When complimenting her — pick out something specific. Don't talk about body parts or how her jumpsuit fits on her ass. Give her a good compliment then quickly move to less romantic conversation before she gets uncomfortable.

Try to get a job where you're under her supervision. Something where you are on the same team or share a mutual goal. This is an ideal way to get physical without being too sexual (Liar). It'll also create a gauge to show that you have long–term potential (Buyer). And, as a Shrewd, doing actual concrete activities fits with her worldview of how relationships should be.

Another great way to connect with the Sage is by talking about how the two of you can contribute to each other's lives. For example, if she has an area of expertise you find interesting, have her teach you what she knows. Most people do have a life after work. Find out what her passion is and put yourself in it.

The interaction may feel a little platonic at times during the first couple conversations, but as long as you were direct about being attracted to her at first, she will perceive it as leading towards a romantic outcome. Be patient, but once you get her alone, don't miss any opportunities to take things to the next level.

Strong eye contact is necessary with Buyers. But don't be too flirty with Liars. Look into her eyes when you talk, and when she talks. She is probably laid back— not a high–energy party girl. The Sage is often intelligent and creative— an artistic type. She may feel like she is an outsider, or not quite like everyone else. This is why she doesn't usually play around with people in social settings.

Adapt to this by having a relaxed and unassuming body language. You are interested in her, but there is no pressure. As you get to know her she'll feel invested. There's no need to rush. No fancy moves, or overly confident posturing. If she can sense you are acting through a persona, she will rule out the possibility of an authentic bond, and thus any further contact with you.

CHAPTER FIFTEEN

THE MILLENNIAL

Personality profile: Buyer/Owner/Shrewd

If any woman your're into has her shit together she's a Millennial woman. She's an optimist, she doesn't wear her emotions on her sleeve, and she has a very healthy, real world approach when it comes to men.

The Millennial might have a boyfriend, but for the most part she's not clingy and is open to having casual fun. If she's not in a relationship she'll most likely to have a few "friends" that she's willing to sleep with. This is good news for you because she's usually willing to try new things.

However, remember that she is a Buyer, and if she likes a guy, she will want to focus on him and develop the relationship. She may even have a boyfriend at the moment. But she is also comfortable with casual fun. If she's not in a committed relationship she will be willing to give you a chance because she's open to trying new things.

She might sound too good to be true, and if you know what you're doing she may be the blessing you've been looking for. In all actuality the Millennial is rather common in today's day in age. More and more women are pushing like her. The level–headed, rational, sexual, yet not too slutty woman is "what's up" these days.

HER CRAVINGS

The reason why a millennial woman is so susceptible to convicts is because she's not looking for someone rich or super successful. What she really wants is someone with a future. Don't forget, she's a Buyer. She'll help you get where you want to go— you just gotta have drive!

Her biggest turn offs are:

1. Selfishness— she has high self–esteem and won't put up with a guy who doesn't value her or treat her with respect.
2. Lack of direction— why would she want to attach herself to a man who is going nowhere?
3. Neediness— if she is attractive, she has men clamoring to get in her pants. If she is cool and confident, she has men also clamoring to be her boyfriend. She has goals, a job/working on her degree, and doesn't have time to babysit other grown–ups.

HER TECHINIEQUES

If she's single she'll let it be known. The Millennial is active, she's talkative and extremely social. All her clothes fit well, hugging all the important curves. Sex is a perk that comes with being "free," so she's open to sexy conversations and peeking at "packages."

Ultimately she wants to meet the right guy, if she hasn't already. She may start to worry about this as she nears or passes the age of 30. But she has enough going in her life to feel good about herself, whether she has a serious boyfriend or not.

A lot of guys in prison are compulsive liars. Telling the

truth is against their morals. Well, something you need to remember about the Millennial is if she catches you lying— it's a wrap. Not only does it mean she can't trust you, but it's also insulting and makes you look fake. The Millennial wants you to be "real!" Be honest about who you are and what you want. Man, if you meet her while you are in prison then she knows what she's getting into, there's no need to lie about shit. Most dudes lie to females because they don't understand them. By being honest and authentic in your dealings with women you will appear bold, confident and knowledgeable about the opposite sex.

POINTS OF CONQUEST

Mouthpiece

As an Owner, the millennial woman is interested in your potential, as well as your level of confidence. The best way to convey both is by being direct and honest in your approach. She likes knowing that you chose her— to a Buyer, your interest in her is exciting. Compliments work really well with this type of woman, but you gotta be smooth. Keep in mind that you're in a setting with 100's of other guys. She's heard all the generic compliments already— be original. And make sure to lock eyes with her every time you step up to the plate!

It's not hard to approach this type of woman because she likes talking to guys. You may at times meet one that is in a bad mood or simply not interested for whatever reason. That's okay, cut your losses and stay positive about the process.

The combination of Buyer–Owner makes her fun to talk to. She likes to talk about sex and responds well to flirting. She can probably hold her own with deeper conversation. The best way to engage her attention is to ask her about how she thinks about the topic. For example, if she tells you she likes baseball, ask her how she got interested in it.

If she tells you that she went out with her friends over the weekend, ask her whose birthday it was, find out how they all met. Ask her what she plans on doing on her vacation break. A good question to ask a Millennial is what kind of music she listens to, and who is her favorite artist. What does she do to relax? Does she have time for hobbies?

CLOSING THE DEAL

Closing the deal with a Millennial is easy as long as you seem genuinely interested in her as a person. At the same time, while asking her questions about herself, interject fun facts about yourself. Tell her stories about your life, or talk about your goals. Can't shrug from sexual topics, either. Tell her what you like about women and be honest — remember, women can smell a fake a mile away.

Most guys in prison are walking around with a chip on their shoulder. Don't show her that. Relax your body and look happy when you're around her. Looking happy doesn't mean walking around with a shit–eating grin on your face, either. It means you light up whenever you're in her company.

CHAPTER SIXTEEN

VERBAL INTERCOURSE

I bet you think this chapter is gonna be about talking dirty to your girl, huh? Sorry, fellas, it's not....

The word intercourse means a connection between two people. Yeah, most people automatically associate it with sex, but that's "sexual intercourse." Anyways, in this chapter I'm going to give you a number of conversation starters that you can/must utilize to get the maximum understanding from your better half.

For lack of a better word, I'll use the term "triggers" when I refer to these conversation starters. These triggers can be used every time you find yourself with writer's block and you need help with fodder for you letters. You can use these triggers during phone calls, visits, or face–to–face interactions. Here's the thing though, these questions aren't designed to kill time. They were created to ignite serious conversation that will allow you to enter someone's mental.

In order for you to be at Master at Communicating you have to know how to listen. Not only are you supposed to listen to what she has to say, but you also need to know the right questions to ask so that you can get the most information. And the purpose for all of this is so you can get to know your prey better than she knows herself.

$$$$$

Here are some questions to help start a conversation with your partner about your relationship. Give thought not only to your responses, but to your partner's responses. You may be surprised at what you discover:

* Why did you choose to date someone in prison?
* What is the best part of your relationship?
* What is the most difficult aspect of your relationship?
* Is having a relationship with someone in prison more or less difficult than your thought it would be? Why?
* What is the most significant potential pitfall you believe you might encounter in this relationship?
* What makes this relationship worth it?

How well we communicate is usually a strong indication of how successful our relationships will be. As you and your partner take turns finishing each of the following sentences, focus on listening to what the other is saying and on providing the clearest possible statements:

* We are most successful in our communication efforts when we...
* Our communication is most difficult when we...
* Sometimes I don't understand what you mean when you...
* At times I feel you don't understand me when I...
* I would feel more confident in our relationship if I heard you say...
* I would believe that you understood me better if you...

Talking to each other about your goals is an important step

you must take if your relationship is to continue moving forward. Use the questions below to facilitate a conversation with your partner about setting mutual goals:

* Where do you see yourself in three months? Six months? A year? How about ten years? How does our relationship fit into those plans?

* What are your plans for marriage and family? How soon do you hope to see those plans come to fruition?

* What personal goals have you established for yourself? How might these affect our relationship?

* What long–term goals would you like to establish for our relationship? How might these impact your personal goals?

* Which aspects of dating a convict do you enjoy? Which do you wish you could change?

* Would you feel the same about me if I were free? Why or why not?

* Would you be willing to move for the sake of our relationship?

*What would you be giving up to move closer to the prison? What do you think your partner would be giving up if she moved near you?

* What would change in our relationship if I were to get out today?

An open discussion is the first step in strengthening trust in relationships. Remember, you and your partner may not always see eye to eye, but by understanding one another and truly caring about each other's feelings, you should be able to reach compromises that make you both happy. Here are some questions to get you started:

* Do you feel you can trust me fully? Why or why not?
* Do you ever feel I may not be telling the truth? Why

or why not?

* How do you feel about the importance of fidelity in a relationship? How would you feel if you were to discover your partner was unfaithful?

* What was your parents' relationship like when you were growing up? Were both parents' faithful? How do you think their relationship has impacted your view of fidelity and trust today?

As difficult as it is, discussing temptation openly is the best way to ensure that you and your partner don't give in to it. These questions will give you a starting point for opening up a conversation with your partner:

* Have you ever felt tempted to stray from your relationship? If so, what was appealing about the idea? Did you follow through on it?

* If you have been faithful, what keeps you from giving in to temptation?

* Have you ever been involved in a relationship in which fidelity was an issue?

What happened? How did it impact your approach toward relationships now?

* Does your current relationship fulfill your needs for companionship and closeness? What creative ways can you and your partner come up with to bring you closer together, in spite of the miles that keep you apart?

* When do you feel most lonely in the relationship? Is there anything you or your partner can do to lessen those feelings of loneliness?

Open up a dialogue with your partner and start working out the best strategies to keep your own relationship feeling real.

The following questions can provide a starting point for discussion, but don't limit your conversation to the topics here. Remember, whatever matters most to each of you individually is what will be most important to maintaining a sense of normalcy in your own unique relationship:

* What does it mean to have normalcy in a relationship?

* What aspect of distance is currently the biggest obstacle in keeping a sense of normalcy in your relationship?

* What parts of our relationship feels real? What parts seem less so? Why?

* What can you each do to help your relationship feel more normal, in spite of prison?

* Do you spend your time together in the best way possible? Could you better use your time to help the relationship feel more genuine?

Use the questions below to open up a dialogue about commitment with your partner:

* What does the word commitment mean to you? Do you view it as a positive or negative word?

* What commitments have you made in your life? Were these commitments easy or difficult, and why? What was the result?

* Do you believe that commitment is appropriate at different levels of relationships? What would commitment look like at different stages of dating?

* Have you ever committed to a romantic relationship in the past? What was the result?
How has that experience influenced the way you view commitment today?

* Do you believe that you're currently committed to me? Why or why not?

* What, in your view, is the ultimate goal of this relationship?

$$$$$

If you take only one thing away from reading this chapter, I hope it's that you must take your time to get know people if you really want to cultivate a real relationship. Nothing comes easy, but you should love doing what you do, so none of this should seem like work.

CHAPTER SEVENTEEN

THE PHONE GAME...

Hmmm... This subject hits kinda close to home with me because I've actually had PTSD from using that state phone. For those of you who've read my How To Hustle & Win: Sex, Money, Murder Edition book, you know that I didn't always have the network or money that I've accumulated with book sales and extracurricular activities. I've gone years without phone calls, mail or visits. When I first went to prison, I fell out–of–state (Florida). So every time I wanted to make a call it would cost 20 dollars. Needless to say, that limited my phone access.

But that's not what I got PTSD from. What fucked me up was all the times I got bad news like a homey getting killed, a family member catching a case, or a baby mamma acting up. Add all that in with the fact that my calls were so expensive that I just learned to dodge that phone.

Nevertheless, when I got into this pen pal game I quickly learned that even though words on paper can move mountains, there's nothing like letting a woman hear your voice. There's something in their DNA that reacts to a man's voice and all of you should cash in on this phenomenon every chance you get.

I always ask for my pen pal's number within the first 3 to 5 letters. Now that these class–action lawsuits have forced the prison phone companies to drop their rates we can call cross country for anywhere from 3 to 5 dollars. If you can get 'em to put 20 dollars on your phone account that should give you enough time to get in their ears to work your magic.

Here are a few tactics you can use to elevate your phone game...

1. Set a day and time to call in advance. Some couples find it necessary to talk every day. Others use daily letters to fill in the gaps between less–frequent phone calls. Planning for the call in advance lets you look forward to the time you will talk, and also ensures you're not in the middle of something else when the call comes. You may even want to designate one specific day and time each week for lengthier phone calls, perhaps on the weekend when her free time is open.

2. Your body language comes out in your voice. Stand up straight so that your whole demeanor sounds confident and powerful.

3. Be witty. Make your friend laugh. Tease her a little, but don't go too hard on her, guys. You don't want to make her cry, bruh.

4. Have a strategy for your phone call. Instead of risking any quiet times on the phone, already have a list of things to talk about.

5. Put aside other activities. Your partner deserves your undivided attention. Chances are, she won't feel too special if you've got all kinds of other conversations going on in the background. Since you see the guys in your building every day, why would you use your phone time to talk to them???

I'd rather talk to a woman over one of these stank–breath dudes any day!

6. Don't interrupt your phone–friend when she's talking. Sometimes all a woman needs is an active listener, so give her that. Let her know you're listening— she'll love it and want you to keep calling back!

7. I know this may sound corny, but use flowery words that describe shit— words like: fantastic, beautiful and great when you're talking to women. Certain words create images in a person's mind, and you want to create bright and happy pictures in her head.

8. Build trust! Never be judgmental. However, women respect a man who respects himself. So, basically, don't be a sucka. Yet, if this is your second phone call and she's telling you about something you don't agree with, don't tell her she's dumb because she doesn't see something the way you do.

9. Never assume someone knows something. Don't talk too fast. Be smooth and let your words resonate. You'll accomplish more this way.

10. If you have to, take a piece of paper and pen with you so you can take notes while you're talking to her on the phone. Pay attention to background noises and at what time of day or night it is happening. You might be able to use this information at a later date.

11. Talk about her letters. There might be times when you can say, "I waited to call you to talk about this certain subject because I feel that talking on the phone would be the best way to express my thoughts on this specific subject."

12. Never call someone when you're mad. Anger is energy in motion, and most of the time the energy is destructive. Keep all of your interactions on a positive note and watch how far you'll get with the opposite sex!

13. Never break up over the phone! It's easy to say and do things while you're not in a person's face. Most of the time, if you are in your girl's face, she wouldn't be acting (out of anger) as hard as she will on the phone. Keep that in mind when you get to the point where you want to end things. If it gets to that point, at least give yourself one last face–to–face visit.

14. Pay attention to phone costs. Not every person has the same amount of resources as the next person. Some of your pen pals will have more money than others, so there will be the ones who can afford to let you call every day, but then again there'll be those who can only afford to accept one call a week. Stay on this, so you don't get the phone cut off.

15. Never, I repeat: NEVER LET ANOTHER PRISONER CALL YOUR GIRL!!! Remember she's "YOUR GIRL", she's not the next man's girl. Always keep in mind that you're in prison. This is a place where they put the grimiest cats of our society. Who's to say that your friend today won't be your enemy tomorrow and you done fucked around and let him have your girl's number??? Real talk!

CHAPTER EIGHTEEN

WHAT I LEARNED FROM GIVING WOMEN PHONE SEX
by David Shade

After my divorce in 1992, I felt very defeated and alone. I had custody of our two small children, and thus, I was stuck at home in the evenings. Hence, after I put the children to bed, I turned to the telephone.

There was a singles magazine in our area where people placed in personal ads. You read through the ads and decided which women to call. You then called a 900 number and left a message and your number. The ladies would then listen to their messages and decide who to call back.

That was back in the days before there was caller ID. The women could call and know that you had no way of knowing who they really were or where they lived, so there was that anonymity which gave them safety.

I picked women who were recently divorced and about 30 years old. When they would call, the rapport would build quickly because we had a lot in common and much to talk about.

I would build common ground based on our similar situations of having gone through a divorce. This allowed her to feel comfortable with me.

I also became very good at establishing an emotional connection with a woman on the telephone. This is critically important. Women are emotional creatures, and they need to establish a connection before they can feel free to continue further.

Since she understood my situation, I would say, "I really enjoy talking to you. I feel like I can tell you anything, and you understand it and accept it." She would reply, "Oh yes, I do!" This served to make her feel that she could tell me anything, as well, and that I would fully understand it and accept it. Thus, she would open up even further.

By the end of their marriage, many of these women no longer felt sexual. They weren't having orgasms, even by masturbating. They didn't even fantasize. There was no point in it.

They had left their marriages for various reasons, but in all cases, the sex had become boring. Their husbands were lousy lovers. I asked these women, "Was it because he had a small penis?" They replied, "Well, actually, no."

Many of them had affairs with exciting lovers. They talked about how much their lover turned them on. I asked them, "Was it because he had a big penis?" They replied, "Well, actually, no."

Apparently, it didn't have anything to do with the size of the man's penis.

All of my preexisting beliefs about sexuality began to crumble.

So far, this may sound as if I was being very pathetic, and as I look back on it, I can see it that way.

However, hearing these women's stories was fascinating to me.

It was also therapeutic for me. It was sort of a "mutually helpful divorce recovery program." It helped me to deal with my recent divorce. Also, I have to admit, it helped with the loneliness.

The women were lonely, too. They were reaching out in the dark to talk to another human being, to have thoughtful human interaction.

For them, it was also therapeutic to share their secrets, even with an anonymous person; and because it was anonymous, they were completely open and honest.

I was learning a lot. The stories were very revealing, and quite fascinating.

I became very good at getting them to open up and share.

I would ask them, "What do you really want in a man?" They would describe, or at least try to describe, what they wanted to the best of their ability. Often, they didn't really know themselves; they just knew what they wanted to feel. The important thing is that they started to feel those feelings while they were on the phone with me.

So, I would then ask, "How would it make you feel to be with such a man?" They would describe that. In order to do so, they had to imagine feeling it. This caused them to actually begin to feel those feelings and imagine that they were really with that man. Because they were talking to me and had rapport with me, those feelings got associated to me on a subconscious level. They did not realize this on a conscious level.

Because I was genuinely interested in what they thought, and because I made it a point to demonstrate that I was a good listener, they opened up about what they would really like to have— in other words, what they fantasized about on an emotional and relationship basis.

When they were basking in a flood of good emotions and feelings, which were all connected to me, I would ramp that up. After having established an emotional connection with them that allowed them to feel very close to me, I leveraged that to move the conversation in a romantic direction.

I would ask them to describe what they would do on the ideal "date." They would describe some romantic night out, consisting of dinner, dancing, and walking on the beach. Of course, they gave me detailed descriptions. "Then, we are seated at our table, which is adorned with a fine white linen tablecloth and one tall candle."

Sometimes, they would instead prefer that I describe, what was told to me by previous women. It's simple really—women want what they have to have.

After they were basking in the flood of romantic feelings, all of which were linked to me, I covertly moved things in a sexual direction.

I would ask, "Do you ever feel alone?" They would affirm.

Then, I posed these questions: "What would it feel like to be opposite of alone? What word could be used to describe that?"

They would try to describe it and put a word to it. It served to remind them that they were alone and how much they yearned to feel close and connected.

Then, I would say, "Yeah. Sometimes I feel alone, especially at this time of night. I think about what it would be like to be with that someone special. What would we say? What would we do? How would we make each other feel?"

They would softly agree, "Yeah..."

Then, I'd continue, "I feel very close to you right now." They would reply, "Yes, I feel very close to you, too."

Then, I would softly say, "I wish I were there with you right now." They would softly reply, "Yes..."

"If I were there right now, I would want to hold you so close." They softly replied, "Yeah..."

"And I would feel your soft skin against mine." They would sigh.

Here is the critical point...

"And I would ever–so–softly kiss the side of your neck."

At this point, 80 percent of the women would simply stop talking and just sigh.

I would continue...

"And I would softly kiss the side of your neck all the way down to your shoulder."

I would slowly describe in detail everything I would do if I were there, beginning with what I would kiss, then what I would touch.

They would moan.

Then, I told them that I would lick.

Within minutes, these women would be screaming in orgasmic ecstasy.

These women were attractive and educated. On the very first call, fully 80 percent of them would engage in phone sex with me, a man they have never talked to before in their life.

$$$$$

Now, think about what you can make happen with a female you've already established a rapport with...

CHAPTER NINETEEN

THEY HAVE THEIR NEEDS TOO...

I'm slightly conflicted on this issue because I want to talk about the fact that your girl (whether you met her in prison, out of prison, or a pen pal website) will eventually "cheat." See, in my eyes, it's not cheating if she sleeps with someone while I'm in prison because I know that sex ain't shit. I understand that total devotion is established in the mind, not the pussy. Nevertheless, a lot of guys operate with their feelings so this subject has to be discussed. What's so cold about this is that nine times outta ten, you were the one doing the unfaithful shit when you were free. But now, it ain't no fun when the rabbit got the gun.

Seriously though, on some real shit; there are always victims, regardless of whether or not the infidelity is discovered. When we aren't faithful to our partner, we cheat ourselves out of ever really knowing just what could develop in a committed, honest relationship. A part of us is always hidden, and that means we can never truly build a meaningful, full connection. Any way you look at it, when a partner is unfaithful,
nobody wins.

This isn't to say it's impossible to move past infidelities in a relationship or to make things work after an affair. Some couples tend to feel that surviving an infidelity actually made their relationship stronger. But one popular philosophy states, "You can't turn a ho into a housewife." Surely, no stereotype is true in every case. But if your partner has cheated on you, be careful. Someone who's been unfaithful once may be more likely to have subsequent affairs, particularly if she feels that there are no real consequences for having been unfaithful.

I think this sort of ambivalence is the unfortunate aftermath of a situation that could have been avoided entirely if both partners were honest with one another from the start. Settling for a relationship where trust is not fully possible compromises the love and commitment everyone in life deserves. If your partner has been unfaithful, it's up to you to choose whether or not to continue the relationship. I can't make that decision for you. But, whatever you decided, I recommend that you think long and hard about the kind of love you deserve (provided that love is in the equation), and about what you want out of a relationship, and if those ideals will ever be fully possible now that your trust has been broken.

So what should you do if you think your partner might be cheating on you? This is a potentially explosive topic, and approaching it too aggressively could lead to an unnecessary and unhappy conclusion. And what that interprets to is if you have a woman who's looking out for you and she had an itch that she had to scratch, you could fuck around and lose everything you've been working so hard to establish. One of the most important things you should remember when dealing with people is that we're all human and we all have needs.

NOW, I'm telling you that I don't trip when my females do they thang while I'm in here (as long as it doesn't affect my issue), but that does not mean I'm telling any of you to let yourself get played. If you think something's up, look into it, and here's a few things to look for:

1. Defensiveness. When you ask your partner where she's been or what she's been doing, a defensive response would indicate your girl has something to hide.

2. Secretiveness. If your partner seems to have a lot of secrets, one of those secrets just may be the one you don't want to hear.

3. Limited availability. If it seems as though your girl is always too busy with work or school or other commitments to make time for you, she just may be making time for someone else. At the very least, this sort of unavailability could indicate that your partner isn't interested enough in your relationship to give it the time and attention it deserves. My advice? Move on.

4. Friends or family you never meet. A faithful partner will have no trouble introducing you to family and friends, because your relationship isn't something to hide. Hesitation to introduce you to the other people in her life usually indicates that either there is uncertainty as to whether or not you are "the one," or someone else may already be in the picture.

5. New friends. Just because your partner starts hanging out with a new crowd doesn't mean that infidelity is in the cards, but don't rule it out. Many people start socializing with new groups of friends when their behavior would be frowned upon by their usual social circle.

6. Mysterious phone calls. A quickly dismissed call while you're on the phone might be an attempt to hide another relationship.

7. Strange behavior on the phone. If your girl seems hesitant to call you by your name or is too busy to talk on the phone, it might indicate that someone else is in the room.

8. A sudden interest in seeing other people. If your girl suddenly starts talking about how it might be time to consider no longer dating exclusively, there's a good chance she may

already not be.

9. Guilty behavior. Sometimes those little surprises— an extra money order, a card or an unexpected package— may be purchased to help clear a guilty conscience. Don't jump to conclusions. A thoughtful gesture may be just that— a thoughtful gesture. But if that gesture comes on the coattails of other strange behaviors, be cautious.

10. A gut feeling that something isn't right. More than anything else, when it comes to detecting infidelity you need to trust your instincts. Avoid overreacting or looking for problems that aren't there, but if you don't feel right in the relationship, your best bet is to talk to your girl about your feelings and find out if they're well founded or not.

CHAPTER TWENTY

25 THINGS YOU MUST DO WHEN WRITING A PEN PAL

1. Make sure your handwriting is legible. How are you going to enter anyone's mental if they can't understand your written thoughts?
2. Put in work. Listen, if you're in a cell all day, there's no reason why you can't write a 2 or 3 page letter to your pen pal. If it's business, 1 page is cool. But if you're on a personal level with your pen pal— make it rich with character and content.
3. Write with the words you talk with. Or, at least use language that the average person can understand. If you try to sound all collegiate and shit you might start using words that you don't even know the definition of, and that's kind a stupid.
4. Check your spelling, playboy! You don't want to throw your pen–friend off in mid thought by spelling a word wrong. Take your time, check with Merriam–Webster...
5. Try to end your pages on cliff hangers. Turn the page while you're in the middle of a paragraph so that your reader will have to rush to turn the page to find out what you wrote.
6. Strive to make your pen pal laugh. You want your friend to smile whenever she sees your letter in her mailbox. You can do this by being a MAC and making her laugh.

7. Keep your missives orderly, stay focused on specific subjects. If you attempt to ask your pen pal to do 15 different things, she'll most likely forget certain things. It's best to keep subject matter down to about three topics. If you have more, write another letter.

8. Be a life coach! Give your pen pals advice that will build on their existence here on earth.

9. Find out what interests your friend and send 'em magazine articles that pertain to that subject. I do this all the time, I take articles out of the free publications that I get.

10. The best way to show that you don't have low self–esteem is to crack jokes about yourself. Tell 'em a few jokes at your own expense and it'll show how down–to–earth you can be.

11. Keep track of birthdays. Invest in a few cards and send them like missiles.

12. Tailor your letters for each individual. I once wrote out a form letter that I "tried" to use on all my new pen pals, and that definitely didn't work out for me.

13. If you want a reply you gotta give the recipient a reason to write back. Ask questions that trigger conversations.

14. Keep your letters about the individual. Don't brag about how many pen pals you have. Without necessarily lying, you may want to make your pen pals think/feel like they are your only pen friend.

15. Keep a happy vibe about yourself. If you start writing negative letters your pen pals will begin to loathe opening your envelopes.

16. Even if your pen pal makes you angry— send a reply written calm and collectively. Remember, this is a game of chess.

17. Tell stories of your past to make a point. In my book How To Hustle & Win: Sex, Money, Murder Edition I used

stories of my street endeavors to teach my readers about the game. There's power in words.

18. Religion... Talk of religion is only good when you meet someone on that footing. Most people aren't fanatics, so if you base all of your letters on that theme you'll end up losing pen pals.

19. Pictures are worth a thousand words. Instead of building up a conceited picture of yourself by always talking about your glutes and abs— send a flick and let the image do the talking for you.

20. Real men don't gossip. There's a difference between telling a funny story about something that happened on the yard, but gossiping is for bitches.

21. If you have to write someone about bad news—start, out with the bad news first. Always end with a chunk of positivity.

22. I like to start my letters with a quote. Quotes make you look smart too. Try it out, it doesn't even gotta come from a famous person. You can quote a character in a book or someone you know.

23. Keep your final thought simple. If your P.S. is longer than a few sentences, maybe your letter wasn't finished yet.

24. If you really are rushed, and you don't have time to send a full length letter, then let your pen pal know that you will sit down and write the first chance you get.

25. Last but not least, take your time. We all know what we want out of these pen pals. With some people it'll take a little longer to reach your goals. Everyone is different so don't put a time limit on what you want to accomplish. Be patient and all your goals will come to fruition!

CHAPTER TWENTY-ONE

SHY GUY'S GUIDE

Shy guy quiz

1. So you're at a party when you spot the most exquisite looking woman you've ever seen. She holds eye contact with you for a moment and then slinks into the kitchen. Do you:

a) Continue chatting with your friends but every so often subtly check the room to see if she's re–entered.

b) Freak out, yell "She looked at me!" and scurry out of the party panting in fear.

c) Interpret her eye contact to mean she loves you and proceed to relentlessly follow her around until she admits it.

2. You're ready to ask your crush out on a first date. You get her contact information and...

a) Call her and say you'd really like to take her out and show her a good time.

b) Think about her as hard as you can so that maybe, through mental telepathy, she'll know you're interested and she'll contact you.

c) Leave her a voicemail, an email, and arrange a singing telegram. You can never be too sure, and plus, you're the greatest, so she'll love all the attention!

3. You're at dinner with a date and the conversation has turned a tad awkward. You:

a) Attempt to make a witty joke about the waiter, hoping it will lighten the mood.

b) Start sweating profusely and berating yourself for your lack of swagger.

c) Blame her for the awkwardness, as you know you're amazing so it can't be your fault.

4. It's the end of the night and all you want to do is kiss her. Her lips are plump and glossy as she says, "Well, goodnight..." You:

a) Gently cradle her face in your hands and ask, "May I kiss you?"

b) Scream "Goodnight!" as you bolt from the doorway, ultimately tripping on your shoelaces.

c) Lean in, pucker up and wait for her to kiss you.

4. Somehow you've scored and gotten her into your bed, although she's not entirely naked.

Do you:

a) Slowly and seductively begin to remove articles of clothing, taking cues from her sounds.

b) Stay fully clothed, begin to sob, and say something to the effect of "Forgive me Father, for I might sin."

c) Remove all of your own clothing and let her revel in the joy that is your body.

ANSWER KEY

IF YOU ANSWERED MOSTLY C's, you're the opposite of shy and this isn't necessarily a good thing. While it's nice to have confidence, you must remember that a little humility goes a long way. Sure, you were told by your mother that you're God's gift to the Earth, but that doesn't mean you should believe it. It's great that you're secure, but it's important to check your ego if you want to have a lasting relationship.

IF YOU ANSWERED MOSTLY B's, you're not just shy, you might actually be certifiable. Remember, they're only women and they can't bite you. Most ladies like a little confidence in their guys, and while you don't have to be aggressive or even ultra–assertive, it is important that you believe in yourself. If you don't, why should she believe in you?

IF YOU ANSWERED MOSTLY A's, you strike a good balance between overconfidence and shyness. You don't come on too strongly, but you also don't run from a challenge. When it comes to approaching women, there are times when your heart beats fast and you get a little hot under the collar. But you never let your fear take over and you know how to play up your strengths. Good job!

MAKING IT WORK

Whether it's passed down, learned; or is just part of your personality, being shy doesn't have to be a death sentence when it comes to the ladies. While feeling socially awkward certainly has its disadvantages— panic attacks when trying to express your feelings, avoiding people or situations so as not to feel insecure — but there are times when being shy can actually work to your advantage. Take a look at some pros of being timid:

1. STRONG, SILENT AND SEXY

MIKE ENEMIGO & KING GURU

Many truly shy folk tend to feel withdrawn in social situations, particularly those that involve strangers. But what you know to be timid, others might perceive as strong, silent and sexy. In other words, your reserved nature may actually turn women on. They may ask themselves, "Why isn't he talking to me? Do I look okay?" You know it's because you're too nervous to talk to them, but they don't know that. So go along with it and play it up.

2. LESS ACTION, LESS DRAMA

By being the guy who's on the sidelines, you can reserve your energy for when it really matters. Perhaps you're not the loudest or the most assertive in public, but your shyness with others could make the intimate times with those you do know and love all the more special.

3. TAKING IT ALL IN

So maybe you're the quiet one at the party, but this doesn't have to be a bad thing. A shy person may be more likely to listen first, then respond, an approach that can be as effective personally as it is professionally. With regard to attracting a woman, putting the 'gentle' in gentleman can be really attractive, often a welcome change form more aggressive approaches to dating.

COME ON, DON'T BE SHY

If you're naturally timid, it doesn't mean you can't do anything about it. Here are three ways to overcome your shyness.

TAKE A BREATH

Your heart's racing, your forehead has become shiny and you need to shut those nerves down. Take some advice from yoga instructors and learn to control your breath. When you feel yourself getting panicked, breathe in through your nose and slowly let the breath out through your mouth as you count to 10. Calming yourself physically can lead to more confidence, which is ultimately super–sexy to women.

OWN IT

Being shy doesn't have to carry negative connotations. Not every guy wants to be the center of attention, nor should he be. Although it might sound like an oxymoron, it is possible to be secure in your shyness. If you're a guy who takes a minute to warm up to a woman you're into, then just accept that you're that kind of guy. The right woman will appreciate who you are at the core. "You may not be the loudmouth or the belle of the ball, but are you thoughtful and sweet? Funny in a quieter way? Focus on your strengths instead of focusing on shyness as a deficit.

KEEP AT IT!

One great way to go from shy to fly is to continue putting yourself into situations you may find awkward or uncomfortable— challenge yourself! For example, say you're worried about getting turned down by a woman, just try her... Start talking, if she turns you away, take it in stride. It didn't/won't kill you, will it? So do it again and again until it becomes second nature.

   Shy or not, remember that hot chicks are only humans, just like you— they're just really, really good–looking ones. Half the time, they're as nervous to talk to you as you are to them. So breathe, stand tall and accept that although you might not be the loudest, you have plenty to offer.

CHAPTER TWENTY–TWO

SEVEN SEX MYTHS

SEX MYTH 1: MOST WOMEN ORGASM THROUGH INTERCOURSE

Freud believed there was something wrong with women who couldn't be satisfied by penetrative sex, but, in retrospect, his notion makes him seem more Nutty Professor than Psychological Superman. Freud's theory has been debunked, big time. The fact is, only about 30% of women can achieve orgasm this way. If your idea of lovemaking consists solely of vaginal penetration, you're denying your honey the full sensory experience she so richly desires. It's really quite simple: The vast majority of women require clitoral stimulation to put them in the kind of euphoric state that has them vocalizing like Jenna Jameson.

The good news is you don't have to search too hard to find it. It's that button–like nub situated just above the opening of her love canal. So always be sure to pay her prawn of pleasure lavish attention with both hands and mouth in addition to the usual in–and–out. Sexologists even recommend less thrusting and more grinding your pelvic bone against hers— to bring her over the edge.

SEX MYTH 2: A WOMAN MUST ORGASM TO ENJOY SEX

It certainly helps, but in the mysterious and labyrinthine realm of female sexuality —which seems only slightly less complicated than Einstein's Theory of Relativity— the orgasm is not the be all and end all. Fact is, many women find sex fulfilling whether or not they achieve orgasm, providing their emotional needs are met. The warmth and intimacy of foreplay— all that kissing, caressing and whispering of sweet nothings — I can often be more satisfying for your partner than the most frenzied love making session. The key, as in most issues between the sexes, is communication. Make a concerted effort to learn about her sexual desires and priorities. Listen to her! Then make a sincere commitment to meeting all of her honey pot needs— emotional as well as physical.

SEX MYTH 3: SOMETHING'S WRONG WITH WOMEN WHO CAN'T ORGASM

This belief, as the English would say, is a load of bollocks. Women who have never had their bell rung may simply never have learned what kind of specific stimulation they need in order to climax. For those who once were able to orgasm but are now denied that pleasure, a medical condition or side effect from certain medications could be the culprit. (The exception is if a woman had what therapists call an "ego dystonic" condition, in which her sexual desires and impulses are in conflict with her self–perception and/or the needs of her ego, which may require treatment.)

SEX MYTH 4: WOMEN WANT SEX LESS THAN WE DO

While it's difficult to define differences between male and female sexual desire with scientific precision, most experts agree that the average, healthy woman's' sex drive is as powerful as a man's. It's just expressed differently. Women generally need a longer period of time to become aroused than men, who can shift into rutting mode quicker than you can say Charlie Sheen. From a physical standpoint, there is no difference whatsoever. Women are known to have orgasms by merely watching a man while they rock their thighs back and forth. It's the social standard in certain cultures that force females to hide their sexual desires that actually fuel this myth.

SEX MYTH 5: WOMEN DON'T CHEAT AS MUCH AS MEN DO

Finally, is it a myth that women are more monogamous than men? Most studies claim that men are more inclined to cheat than women. Twice as likely is the figure the studies use. Are women really behaving themselves when it comes to cheating? Back in the Stone Age, women would cheat with other men to get either more meat or protection. They needed the extra food to feed their children and the protection to keep them safe from predators. Today, women can make all the money they want for whatever they want. Now that women are more economically powerful, they are getting just as adulterous as men, according to current studies. In recent polls, about 51% of women say they are more monogamous and about 49% say they aren't. The myth has finally been exposed!

SEX MYTH 6: NOT ALL WOMEN HAVE A G–SPOT

A German MD first theorized about this in 1950. However, a

recent Italian study using ultrasound scans identified anatomical variations in women who have vaginal orgasms, has lent credence to the growing consensus that the spot exists, but that not every woman has one. This wonderful part of the female anatomy is located approximately a third of the way up on the anterior (front) wall of the vagina— the slightly rough area just behind the pubic bone. It is best stimulated using two fingers on it in a gentle "come hither" motion. Try it on your partner and see how she response. But don't focus so much attention on her G–spot that you overlook the clitoris, which triggers most female orgasms.

SEX MYTH 7: WOMEN DON'T EJACULATE

Don't make any wagers on this one. In addition to vaginal lubrication, women have an ejaculate that can manifest during intense sexual stimulation, usually as a result of pressure on the G–spot, and often in conjunction with multiple orgasms. The source of this femme fluid is the urethra, and it varies from woman to woman— from a gentle trickle to a raging flood tide. Don't freak out if this happens the first time you play bed boogie with a new conquest. Just be happy she's havin a good time.

CHAPTER TWENTY-THREE

SEVEN THINGS EVERY MAN SHOULD KNOW ABOUT BREASTS

By: Cecily Knobler

1. BOOBS ALONE MIGHT GET HER THERE!

Did you know that some lucky women can actually have an orgasm simply from breast stimulation alone? Yep, some ladies are able to get so aroused when you fondle their breasts that they're able to bring it all the way home to the land of eureka. But, guys, don't worry if you're unable to make this happen. While it is possible, it's far from a sure thing. Either way, it can be a lot of fun trying, and with the right combination of touching, she'll love you for it!

2. LACTATION, LACTATION, LACTATION!

One of the first things you may have learned firsthand shortly after entering this world is that most women's breasts produce milk after the baby has arrived. But here's something you may not already know. Some women don't need to bear a child in order to lactate; sometimes all it can take is a certain form of stimulation of the nipples! That's right: Since lactation is caused by pituitary hormones, it isn't necessary that a woman have a child in order to produce milk. Quite a lot of nipple stimulation or message will usually be required to cause lactation, but sucking on the nipples a few times a day coupled with appropriate squeezing of the breasts might be enough to do the job. Not surprisingly, some men get really turned on by the idea of breast milk! But if you choose to go this route, remember to take it easy, boys. Boobs can get super sore, super quickly when there's extra suckling, so make sure she's into it before giving into this liquid fetish.

3. A BIT NIPPY, NO?

The nipple is a sensitive subject, as many nerves lay adjacent to one another just below the surface. But much like the overall breast, the degree to which a woman's nipples might feel good to your touch will vary greatly from woman to woman. Some women sense very little sexual arousal when their nipples are touched and prefer that men focus on the breasts themselves (particularly the sides, which lead under the arm).

But for women who do get turned on by nipple stimulation, there are all kinds of fun ways to enhance the nip–play, For those who like it a little softer, you can of course gently lick the nipples, and for those who like things a tad more rough, a light biting can sometimes be pleasurable.

4. A SORE SUBJECT

I know many of you guys might find this tough to believe, but not all of us women like or want to have our boobs squeezed to the point of deflation. We know you get excited when you see them, but try to keep in mind that breasts are not your personal stress balls. While many women enjoy having them fondled, the globes of your obsession can be sensitive, especially a week or two before a gal's menstrual cycle begins. Each woman's preference for degrees of boob–squeezing varies, even day to day. What may have worked on Saturday night may have the opposite effect on Wednesday. Start out easy and work yourself up to the ultra–squeeze, and please, guys, pay attention to the cues your lover gives you (she might be in pain...)

5. AREOLA, I BARELY KNOW YA!

Surrounding the nipple, in both men and women, is a circular colored area, which varies in size, shape and color. Called the areola, this area can range from tiny to large and from dark brown to light pink to even a pale yellow.

For many women, thanks to the vast array of nerve endings, this area can be quite sensitive. The size or color of the areola, however, does not affect the level of sensitivity.

It all comes down to personal preference and if your companion is someone who likes attention paid to this area during sex, you should definitely go for the gusto. In fact, during foreplay, it's a great place to start before attempting to stimulate the even more sensitive nipple: As a foreplay technique some couples even like smearing the area with honey or chocolate and then licking it off. An ice cube can also be exciting, although I'd advise against keeping it on the breast for very long, as you want to arouse your lover, and not turn them into a pair of Arctic angel cakes!

6. THE REAL DEAL OR MAN MADE?

Well, it's no secret that not all boobs out there are exactly entirely natural. Whether it's due to extreme social pressures or to personal preference, some women prefer to have their breasts enlarged.

NOW, it's important to note that a woman who decides to enhance her breasts shouldn't be judged for her decision, and while it's okay for you to have a preference between real or augmented, it's not okay for you to make a woman feel bad about her choices. Putting it bluntly, if you had a small Johnson and could make it any size you wanted, wouldn't you consider it too? Of course, this goes both ways, and if your girlfriend has what are considered smaller cups, it's your job to let her know they're beautiful just the way they are, because they are beautiful. Don't pressure her to meet your own needs, and know that getting implants is still very much a real surgery, with attendant risk that should be seriously considered.

7. MEN HAVE BOOBS TOO!

Well, let's just go there. Boys have breast tissue too, just like girls. With women, it's the hormones during puberty that lead to breast "development" into the pretty little things they are. But there are some boys, who, due to hormonal imbalances, themselves develop larger breasts, which some have termed "man–boobs," can be caused, even in a man's later years, by excess body fat or the use of certain medications. In fact, those who use a lot of testosterone and steroids readily tend to develop the condition, which is medically referred to as gynecomastia.

CHAPTER TWENTY–FOUR

7 SECRETS TO KEEP WOMEN INFATUATED WITH YOU!

1. Women in general don't really expect much from guys. Most guys don't know how to impress a woman so women don't anticipate or expect to be awed by men. Every now and then go the extra mile for her and do it in a big way. When you're together, listen to what she says and pay attention to what she really likes. Take note of something she sees in a store that she really likes and go back later to buy it for her. Women who feel grateful for their partner's kind action are extremely impressed and have much stronger bonds than those who don't.

2. Improve your communication skills and it will boost your sex life. Forget being the strong silent type; it will get you nowhere and she'll never be smitten with you if you do. Women feel a greater intimacy with men who are open about their feelings and keep the communication going throughout the relationship. When a woman knows that you trust her enough to be open and vulnerable around her, she becomes more passionate and more connected to you.

3. You can control her mind with her own hormones. When

women become smitten with a man their brain takes on a whole process of activity in the caudate section. That's the area of the brain responsible for cravings. Her brain will start producing dopamine, which is a powerful neurotransmitter. There is also a chemical called oxytocin, which is produced in the pituitary gland that promotes sexual arousal in women. It also produces feelings of attachment in women. Your job is to stimulate these hormones by touching and cuddling with her as much as possible. Also having sex with her as much as possible will produce these same chemicals.

4. Here you show her how smitten you are with her and in return she will not be able to resist becoming love–struck with you. Most guys won't do this because they think it's not very masculine, but women love being irresistible. Showing her that she's enticing and downright mouthwatering will make her feel special and wanted and in return, will make her feel the same about you.

5. Build rock–solid trust by always talking her up no matter where you are or whom you're with. You could be at a party or a wedding or just around her family. Don't be afraid to tell everyone just how great she is. No matter what the subject of conversation is at the moment. It could be about her job for instance. Tell them how great she is at it, or how devoted she is to her workouts at the gym. Once she gets wind form her friends
and family that you have been talking her up in front of them, she will love you and want you like you won't believe.

6. Start talking more in the bedroom. Communication in the bedroom is key to making her sex life number one. Ask her what she wants. Go for total openness. Once you get to know what she really likes you will have much more explosive sex

than you ever imagined. Every woman is different. Don't base what you have done to other women as a gauge to what you are going to do to her. A touch that's great and orgasmic for one woman may not feel like anything to another. So listen to how she likes her clitoris to be touched. That's one part of the woman's anatomy that has more nerve endings than your penis. Only she knows how it feels, so learn it her way.

7. Always make a memorable entrance when you know she's going to be there. The first thing a woman notices about a man is how he enters a room. If you do it right you will be incredibly sexy to her forever. Right before you open the door or enter the room take a deep breath and exhale gently, tighten your stomach and look as symmetrical as possible. Look fit and healthy. Buy clothes that make you look good no matter if you think she will like it or not. Dress for you, not what you think she would like to see.

CHAPTER TWTENTY–FIVE

OVER–STANDING YOUR CIPHER

My definition of a cipher is any person, place, or thing. Any situation I am a part of or about to step into is a cipher. A cipher is also a circle of energy, so this whole realm of women and pan pals is a cipher within itself.

Over–standing is another way of saying the word understanding. I call it over– standing because I have learned to grasp the power of words. When you have reached an understanding of something it means you've studied the ins and outs of it and you've reached a full level of comprehension. Well, if this is the case then why call it "under"–standing? Wouldn't the proper phrase be "over"–standing?

Whenever I write an essay, chapter, or book on something I make it a point to put out real facts, real game, and real knowledge. I do this because I thrive to have an impeccable reputation in all of my endeavors. Nevertheless; and I can't emphasize this enough: Never just take someone's word at face value! When a person gives you their perspective on a certain cipher your first step should be to do your own research on said subject.

Whether you have to read some more books, or have someone google something for you— do it! Study what I tell you by looking for information through other sources. If you can't find sources of information then use your own wisdom to come up with your own take on things. Mike (Enemigo) just had some internet searches sent to me that I want to share with y'all in case you don't have the resources to do it yourself. The following articles are called:

Dating a Prisoner: What Attracts People on the Outside to fall in Love with a Convicted Criminal, by Sharon Murphy, and An Expert Reveals the Psychology Behind Women Who Love Men Behind Bars, by Taylor Bell

Consider these articles as part of your research into the cipher you're looking to enter. Both of them are extremely insightful, and will give you a level of over–standing that will elevate your mental.

$$$$$

DATING A PRISONER: WHAT ATTRACTS PEOPLE ON THE OUTSIDE TO FALL IN LOVE WITH CONVICTED CRIMINALS, by Sharon Murphy

When looking for a partner, the majority of women cite good sense of humor as an essential requirement. And in the shark infested world of online dating, we assume their only experience of porridge to be the kind found on the breakfast table. Not so for the increasing number of ladies who write to strangers in prison.

Prior to the internet, prison pen pals relied on snail mail. However, in recent years, the advent of websites such as MeetaPrisoner.com, InmatesForYou.com, and even GayPrisoners.net have made it easier for people to connect with potential suitors on the inside. Whilst prevalent in the States, each facility differs as to what they allow or disallow, but the general rule is that anything being sent to or from an inmate goes through a screening process. In the UK, people who wish to write letters to inmates can do so via www.prisonerspenfrinds.org.

Prisoners in the UK have no direct access to social media or the internet in general, and letters are still the preferred means of communication. Alex Cavendish, Social Anthropologist and former prison inmate says, "In theory, a percentage of all outgoing letters are randomly checked by the censor's department in each prison (usually 10). However, if the inmate has been convicted of domestic violence, a sexual offence or stalking/ harassment, then all letters are supposed to be read."

Although there are no official figures recorded on the number of letters sent, according to The Office for National Statistics, a report released only this year on population in UK prisons notes 81,881 men compared to 3,882 women currently residing in jail.

Most of us struggle to identify with the type of woman who would actively search for a partner in prison. We read the sensational stories in the Press which tend to veer between pity and disdain. Are they lonely creatures in search of emotional dependence from a captive audience? Or manipulated sociopaths living vicariously through 'celebrity' prisoners?

Fatema Saira Rehman, the woman who wrote to and later married notorious lifer Charles Bronson, once said of her correspondence; "I never expected anything. I thought to myself, he's probably got so many women writing to him, he'll throw it away because it doesn't mean a thing. And I'll go on being a lost soul.

"Cavendish believes it to be a highly complex issue and agrees that major factors to consider are dependency and control; "Dependence works both ways— financial for many prisoners, particularly those who don't have family ties, as well as emotional."

With regards to the type of women who write to prisoners; "I'll be honest and say that a fair few of the female correspondents are lonely women who often have body–image concerns. They feel perhaps that a prisoner is likely to be less judgmental and more appreciative of any support—emotional and/or financial."

For these women, connecting with a man who is locked up for the majority of the day with little else to occupy his time, you'd be forgiven for assuming that the inmate has no choice but to remain faithful. However, as Cavendish observes, prisoners can benefit fiscally from these courtships; "I've known male inmates who have several pen pals, and they live a very comfortable life inside on the regular postal orders or checks that get sent in. I've met straight young prisoners who are keen to find male 'sugar daddies' willing to fund their tobacco or drug habits whilst inside."

Yet it would be wrong to claim that all inmates exploit the situation and all pen pals on the outside are lonely and looking for love.

Many women choose to reach out simply to provide friendship and compassion to those behind bars. Their actions provide a much welcome lifeline, a window to the outside world.

Yet even in platonic cases the lines can get blurred. Georgina Rigby was 28 and working in the field of drug misuse when an inmate contacted her. "He wasn't a direct client, but I recalled him living on the same estate where I grew up. It was platonic at the beginning. I think at first he genuinely wanted someone to talk to, and as the letters progressed they did become more sexual... I could tell that having a sympathetic woman to write to made him feel good and no doubt gave him some fantasy material. As for me, I guess I felt wanted and liked.

"Thinking about it now, several years later, the letters allowed me to be intimate at a distance. To be my 'best self' without the physical and personal flaws that he'd encounter face to face."

For those who instigate and sustain a relationship with a man imprisoned for a lengthy period of time, physical contact is obviously limited, they often never progress beyond the courting stage. As observed by Clinical Psychologist Dr. Stuart Fischoff, "The love object is almost irrelevant at this point. He's a dream lover, a phantom."

However, there are those who do succeed in establishing a 'real life' relationship with the stranger they've connected with. It does occur— but as Cavendish points out, these instances are rare. "There are just too many variables, including license conditions that severely restrict most offenders from starting new relationships or moving their place of residence until their license has expired. In most cases this period can be half of the original sentence— or for life in the case of life sentenced prisoners."

In the UK prisoners can also be placed on a home detention curfew, be expected to permanently reside at a pre–approved address and need to obtain prior permission for a stay of one or more nights at a different address. All continuing with one that began from behind bars.

In short, the fantasy of these type situations rarely match the reality. Similarly there are women who are fascinated with writing to an 'A' list prisoner, those who make misguided attempt to understand the man behind the monster. Their motivation is born from compassion, low self–esteem or ill–advised intentions. However there are others who are attracted to men who commit extreme acts of violence, such as rape or murder.

Hybristophilia is described as a condition whereby women are sexually aroused by and responsive to the men who commit heinous crimes. Often referred to as the 'Bonnie and Clyde Syndrome.'

In this instance the Passive Hybristophile will often contact someone in prison— someone that they only know by reputation in the media. As in the case of Ian Huntley, the notorious Soham killer, he still attracts intense media attention and interest from women on the outside. In reference to Huntley, one such woman, Joanne Rutledge, is quoted as saying; "He's had thousands of letters since he got convicted but I'm the first stranger he's contacted."

More recently during the Oscar Pistorius trial, hordes of women could be witnessed calling out support to him on a daily basis— something I observed personally when watching the news reports.

And perhaps most baffling is the case of Lostprophets singer Ian Watkins. Despite the fact he pleaded guilty a number of sexual assault charges against children, several women have since written to him in jail. One such fan, devastated at the guilty verdict, reportedly said, "He brought so much meaning the lives of his fans that without the Losprophets we're empty. I am in touch with female fans who have written to him sending pictures, telling him they'd wait for him when he is released."

Since he was jailed, deluded supporters set up and regularly contribute to Facebook groups. And although they are frequently taken down, the fans remain active in voicing their support.

Perhaps it's all down to perception. What motivates any of us when it comes to attraction? It's easy for an outsider to make judgement calls, but in the end we all seek relationships which provide us with emotional fulfillment, irrespective of route.

$$$$$

AN EXPERT REVEALS THE PSYCHOLOGY BEHIND
WOMEN WHO LOVE MEN BEHIND BARS, by Taylor
Bell

Charm, intelligence, a solid career are all things women
typically look for in a partner. But for some women, it's the
men locked away in prison who really get their heart
thumping.

Throughout the years women have been attracted to men
behind bars. In fact, California serial killer Richard Ramirez,
convicted killer Charles Manson, along with northern
California killer Scott Peterson have all received marriage
proposals in prison despite their heinous crimes. And with the
introduction of prison pen pal websites such as
PrisonPenPals.com, ConvictMailbag.com,
MeetAninmate.com, women can communicate easily with
prison inmates.

In the book "Women Who Love Men Who Kill," author
Sheila Isenberg explores this phenomenon. The book contains
countless interviews with women, psychiatrists, lawyers,
social workers and prison guards in hopes of shedding light on
why women are drawn to men behind bars.

The book has been featured on CNN, the Today Show,
MSNBC, Good Morning America, and 20/20, among other
news outlets.

BELL: I had a chance to interview Isenberg to talk about
her book and interviews with these women. Here's what she
had to say.

BELL: Were there any commonalities you found with
the women who were attracted to men in prison?

ISENBERGE: The real crux of the whole thing is that
these are all women who are damaged. In their earlier lives
they've been abused either by their parents, their fathers, their

first husbands, and their boyfriends, whatever. They've been sexually abused, psychologically, emotionally abused. These are women who've been hurt. And when you're in a relationship with a man in prison, he's in prison. He's not going to hurt you. He can't hurt you. So you're always in a state of control because you're the one who's on the outside. You're free. You go in and you visit him. You can decide whether to accept his collect phone calls. So in a way, even though cons are very manipulative— that's why we call them con men and they are manipulative with the women— it's still up to the woman to decide how far she wants to go and she knows she can't be hurt.

And every single woman I interviewed had been abused in the past and that's what I found out. That was the big secret.

BELL: What were the demographics of the women you interviewed?

ISENBERG: They came from all different backgrounds, different socioeconomic classes, and different levels of education. They were highly educated women— one woman had a Ph.D. and was a college professor. Other women hadn't graduated from high school. Socioeconomic— there were rich women. There were poor women. There were women who are married, women who were single, women with children, women who didn't have children, all different kinds of women. The only thing they had in common, which I did notice as a common factor, was that there were a lot of Catholic women.

BELL: Did the women feel satisfied in their relationships with inmates?

ISENBERG: The women were generally as they described it, madly in love. They had fallen in love in a way that made them not see the world around them anymore. You know, it's what I call 'stage one super romantic love.' That's the way they saw it. It's the kind of mad, passionate love that makes you lose your appetite, that makes you want to dance and sing. When you first meet someone and you're high as a kite on that person— they all used that language. 'I'm falling in love.' 'I was blinded by love.' 'I felt like I was falling off a cliff.' And that was the initial reaction. That high, that capital 'R' romantic love was kept up during the course of the relationship because the men were in prison, because they could not have a normal life with them. Nobody came home after work and took off his dirty socks and left them on the floor. Nobody came home after work and took off his dirty socks and left them on the floor. Nobody said, 'Oh, I forgot to pick up the laundry.' Nobody said, 'You take care of the kids tonight, I'm tired.' It was none of the normal give and take of a marriage or a live–in companion relationship. It was always, 'Will there be a lockdown?' 'Will they let me in to see him?' 'What's his lawyer going to say?' 'Will he get paroled?' All these dramatic, super dramatic, melodramatic things.

And of course, visiting someone in a prison where you're surrounded by razor wire and high brick walls and mean–looking guards makes your relationship almost like Cinderella and the prince—everybody's out to get you. They're trying to keep you apart. It's very dangerous. It's so romantic. So having a relationship with a man in prison like that for murder is almost like reading a romance novel where you never knows what's going to happen next. You never know if they'll let you into the prison or they're on lockdown or what's going to happen.

BELL: Did these women feel guilty that they were in a relationship with someone who has committed a terrible crime?

ISENBERG: Most of the women I interviewed managed to find a way to rationalize a way or mitigate the crime and excuse it; "He didn't really necessarily mean to be that murderer." There was even one woman I interviewed who was a juror on a jury that convicted a guy of murder and then she went to visit him in prison and fell in love with him.

And afterward she said, "You know, he wasn't really guilty and I don't know why I convicted him." They find ways to excuse the murder. Like one woman I remember she said, "He was awkward and when the door hit him in the arm, the gun went off." Another one said, "His friends were all drinking and doing drugs and he got carried away and he didn't mean to do it."

This story is not in my book but if I was going to write a sequel this would have been in the book. It was a young woman, and this young guy murdered her grandmother. And for some reason she started corresponding with him because she wanted to understand what kind of person could murder a defenseless, little old lady. And she ended up getting involved with him. And I said to her on the phone, "How could you do that? I mean, didn't you feel angry" She said: "He's a changed man. He's not the same person he was." That's another big one: "He did it but he's not the same person." "He found God." "He found religion." Or, "He's sorry."

BELL: How do these women get in contact with these men?

ISENBERG: Back when I wrote the book, it was published in 1990, there was no internet, so it was pretty organic. The women who got into relationships were generally either women who worked in prisons— guards or teachers or lawyers. Some of prison lawyers got involved. There's a girl's famous story which is about a lawyer who got involved with her client and she helped him escape. So that was organic. And then there were also pen pals. Somehow prisoners could get ads in magazines and women wrote to them. I guess they were lonely or whatever. But now, today, we have prison pen pal websites and women can go to those websites and find men to communicate with.

BELL: Unlike the women you interviewed, other women purposely seek out criminals of great notoriety. Why do you think some women pursue a relationship with men who have committed famous crimes?

ISENBERG: We live in a society where we have people who are famous for being famous, like the Kardashians. And when I wrote the book we didn't even have people like that. I think the first person like that was Paris Hilton. She was famous for being famous. So now being famous is even more desirable then when it was when I wrote the book. So how are you going to get famous if you can't make someone on social media read your blog or go to your Instagram or go to your Facebook page. You're not going to get famous by writing a letter to Brad Pritt because he's not going to answer you. But if you write a letter to the Boston Marathon bomber, he might answer you. So it's a very logical way to get famous.

BELL: Was there anything that shocked you about these women?

ISENBERG: What shocked me is the huge numbers, how common it is, how these guys have women all over the place. Your notorious killers have groupies. And now with social media, every one of us who gets involved emotionally with another person, we're doing it to fulfill our own psychological needs. And with the women I interviewed, they were all damaged goods, basically. Their needs were such that they couldn't really find satisfaction or get their needs met in a normal healthy relationship. They had to find love behind the prison walls....

On the Show And Prove tip, I've a got a letter from my Moon in Germany. I met this pen pal when she answered my ad on WriteAPrisoner.com, and she's been on the team for over a year. The following is a group of answers to questions that I sent her for this specific project. This is the glimpse into the mind of the type of females you'll meet while reaching out into the free–world:

"Hey, Baby, here the answers to those questions you sent me...

1. I am 32 years old.

2. I have had pen pals since I've learned how to write. I think I was around ten years old when I got my first pen pal. Of course they weren't prison pen pals, though. It wasn't until about ten years ago that I met my first prison friend. He was on Texas' Death Row.

3. I have always loved to read and write, and I was looking for someone who was willing to have deep, meaningful conversations using pen and paper. While I was growing up, the internet took over and no one was willing to write letters anymore. Then one day a colleague at work motivated me to try to write somebody in prison.

4. I met my first pen pal through a prison pen pal website. But over the years I've met other guys through people who introduce us.

5. When I look at a profile on the internet, the first thing I do is look at the picture. I love to see a smile, I look at their eyes, I try to see whether that man takes care of himself or not. Then I read his text (bio), and I already decided whether I want to meet him before I read what he's about, what his expectations are, what his goals are....

The last thing I look at is their details like age, hometown, skin color, religion, because all that isn't very important to me. The crime they're in prison for doesn't really matter to me because I truly believe in second chances. But I do know that some women care about crimes because they've told me. Some women are very religious and would never write a man who is in prison for rape. Some women are curious and eager to talk to murderers, though. Others have experienced gang violence so they'll never write a gang member. I can only encourage everyone to be honest about themselves and their past.

6. A turn–off for me is pictures where the guy is half naked, and the feeling that the man is looking for financial support. Of course there is nothing wrong in searching for intimacy or money, but both aren't what I am looking for.

7. The shortest time I've written someone is two or three letters, the longest was a period of several years.

8. Yes, I get an immediate feeling inside on the subject of whether or not there's a connection with us. I want to become excited, I want to know that we have a lot in common and a lot to talk about.

9. I prefer writing lifers, people on Death Row, or those with a lot of time because I like to give hope to those who don't have much. I like to give support to those who don't have anyone looking out for them.

10. I enjoy sexual letters when I know there's a connection with the person whom I'm writing. What I hate is when sex is all that we talk about. That gets boring real fast. I want well rounded and balanced communication.

11. Most guys in prison write about their religion, or about how regardless of their predicament, they are truly good people. A lot of them tell me about how lonely they are.

12. Once again, the most important thing is; be honest. Be honest about you, your past, your future, the things you expect, things you don't want. Tell me if there's certain topics that you don't like to talk about, or if there are things you do want to talk about. Be you...

$$$$$

This just came from a female in my cipher. These were comments from a woman who's been writing inmates/convicts for over a decade. So take what you will from it, because it's real thoughts from a real woman.

CONCLUSION

So, we've reached the end of this TCB journey. I'm sure that if you've read every page of this book, you're walking away from it with a fantastic over–standing regarding the pen pal game, and how to crack a female (MAC) while you're in prison. All you gotta do now is put this knowledge to the test.

As I was putting this project together I knew it was going to be more of a guide, or text book, than something you just read once. I set it up for anyone who buys it to be able to set it on their desk and constantly go back to as a reference guide whenever the time calls for it. The letters and poems alone will keep this book in your hand when it's time to sit down and write a letter.

But then it gets deeper with the psychological profiles of all the different women you'll come in contact with. NOW, in the chapters that contain the face–to–face advice, you'll also find jewels that you can also utilize during letter writing sessions, or phone calls with women on the streets. That's how I set it up, and its how you should use the information you come across. The best advice I can give you is to study whenever you choose to seduce a specific woman. Look for her psychological profile, or at least the one that best fits her character attributes. When you find it, study it, but don't forget to improvise when the time calls for it. Not all women are the same. And they will surprise you.

Yes, this book contains the tools to elevate your current status in prison. If you use the things you've read in these pages you'll seduce more women than you would without this information. That's a fact. You'll have different women sending you money, answering your collect phone calls, and coming to visit you. However, if I can get you to take one thing away from everything in this book it is that the power to make your life better lies within you. It's definitely true that a person who is devoted to you can make your life better, yet, the truth is that it's ultimately up to you!

My definition of freedom is to have a FREE DOME; which means a free mind. I refuse to allow these prison walls to keep me down. No one I fucks with let's this prison shit affect them either. My cipher is filled with men who think like me. We might not always agree on everything, but the main thing we all know is that freedom is a state of mind.

Another notion I want to express is that "One monkey don't stop the show." What that translates into is that you shouldn't attach yourself so closely to another human being that if that person (for whatever reason) leaves you for dead, it makes you second–guess your manhood. That's called co–dependency, and a lot of men suffer from it. I've seen way too many guys who walk around prison yards thinking they're Ballers, all because they got a bitch looking out for 'em. Then when that girl leaves 'em, and their funds disappear, those same guys go through a downward spiral. They catch SHU terms, end up hating women, and inherit a fucked up disposition in life.

Everything I write about comes from a personal experience, or that of someone who I've been close to at one time or another. So, when I tell you about things that could happen (downsides), it's not to knock someone who's going through it. It's not to hate on those of you who are at the top of your game. NO! All this is wise words being written. Wisdom.

If you lose a pen pal or girlfriend, don't let it get you down. Get back on your grind and keep MAC'n! The game never stops!

The Cell Block has everything a real convict needs to kick things off! Mike Enemigo has his Resource Guide <u>The Best Resource Directory For Prisoners</u>, out, and that book has every organization prisoners need to make moves happen from the inside of their prison cell. How do I know this? Because I'm living proof; we're living proof of it. My <u>How To Hustle & Win: Sex, Money, Murder Edition</u> book breaks down the game on the streets for all of you who'll be hittin' the bricks soon. NO, it's not gonna teach you how to write a resume, but it will give you insight on the way the underworld works from someone whose pushed weight throughout the United States. Mike Enemigo has several how–to–get–money books. They'll show you how to think like a business man and turn your prison cell into the office of a CEO. All these books accentuate one another.

It's like we're all part of a secret society of go–getters, and all of our secrets are plainly laid out in these books I've just mentioned.

If you can get someone to go on Facebook, Snapchat, or Instagram, look us up! Maybe once you see the Vlogs and pictures of how we're really living inside of these level 4 prisons then you'll know for yourself that everything that comes from The Cell Block is authentic. Maybe that's what it'll take for some of you to wholeheartedly follow our advice and finally start getting everything life has to offer.

Positive Energy Always Creates Elevation, that's PEACE!
King Guru

Christian Pen Pals
PO Box 11296
Hickory, NC 28603

Christian Prison Pen Pals
P.O. Box 333
Inverness, FL 34451

Personal ads start at $10. Send
SASE for complete info.

ChristianPrisonPenPals.org

Post your profile immediately,
just like any dating website, and
edit it any time of day or night.
Friends and family can register,
pay for your ad with PayPal,
and upload your photos,
address, description and bio

Diversified Press
PO Box 135005
Clermont, FL 34713

This company offers a pen pal
page, customized greeting cards
and more. They are willing to
accept stamps as payment.
Write/Send SASE for more
information.

DRL
PMB 154
3298 N. Glassford Hill Rd,
Suite 104
Prescott Valley, AZ 86314

This company offers a pen pal
service with a lifetime
membership for $40.

Write/Send SASE for more
information.

Friends & Lovers Magazine
Luigi Spatota
Suite 46 McCreary Trail
Bolton, Ontario L7E 2C9
Canada

This is a pen pal magazine.
Write for details.

Girls and Mags
3308 Rte. 940; Ste. 104–3018
Mt. Pocono, PA 18344

50 verified mega church
addresses who offer pen pals:
only $8.98 with sample letter.
67 churches that offer a mix of
FREE publications: $6.00 or 20
F/C stamps. 200 pen pal
addresses off the interweb
(some photos and over half
USA); $19.98.

Write your favorite celeb for
FREE photos! Choose from
models, athletes, TV stars,
musicians: $10.00 per list or 3
for $25.00. Each list contains
75 addresses.

600 FREE magazines: Brand–
new exciting catalog of
magazines you may order
FREE! Verified snail mail
addresses and complete
directions. Huge variety (80
pages): $15.98.

New female pen pal ads! With bio and color photos. 100 recently posted Latina Lovers. 100 just posted Black Beauties: $12.00 each.

44 verified pen pal magazines who offer free pen pal ands by snail mail: $14.00 each. Just posted 130 Asian Angels: $12.00. 329 mixed overseas: $18.00.

Comment: Girls and Mags is a new company by George Kayer. George is the founder of Inmate Shopper. He's now retired from Inmate Shopper and has sold it to Freebird Publishers. George is a true hustler, and I have a tremendous amount of respect for that. — Mike

Help From Beyond Walls
POB 185
Springvale, ME 04083

This is a prisoner services company that does it all: pen pals ads, stamp reimbursement, photo editing, gift ordering, internet reach, letter forwarding, website creation and much more. Write/Send SASE for more information.

Human Rights Pen Pal Program
1301 Clay Street, PO Box

71378
Oakland, CA 94612

This is an all–volunteer group that will put you on their list for a pen pal. However, it may take a while, so please be patient.

Inmate Alliance, LLC
PO Box 241
Lebanon, OR 97355

Your pen pal connection. Send SASE for more info.

Comment: Some new shit I ain't checked out yet. But I will. — Mike

InmateConnections
465 NE 181 St. #308
Portland, OR 97230

Pen pal company that runs the sites inmateconnections.com and convictpenpals.com. Send SASE for **FREE** brochure.

InmateNHouse love .com
4001 Inglewood Ave. Suite 10
Dept. 144
Redondo Beach, CA 90278

Pen pal Company. Send SASE for details.

Inmate Classified
PO Box 3311
Granada Hills, CA 91394

This is a pen pal website. They also offer email forwarding. Write/Send SASE for more information.

Inmateconnections.com
465 NE 181st Ave. #308
Portland, OR 97230–6660

Pan pal hookups for prisoners! 92% response rate in 20141 75,000+ hits daily! A+ rating with the BBB! Accepts checks, credit cards, stamps, Moneygram and Trugram. Write for a **FREE** brochure/application. Send SASE or stamp for fast reply.

Inmate–Connection.com
PO Box 83897
Los Angeles, CA 90083

"Only the best and hottest photos! We have the newest, most sensational and exclusive photos on the planet! To order our **FREE** catalog, send SASE or $1.20. All photos are prison friendly. All photos are 4X6, high quality and glossy!

Photo prices:

12 photos for $10
16 photos for $15
22 photos for $20
28 photos for $25
35 photos for $30
45 photos for $35

Minimum order is $10. Additional pics with any set are $.80 each. Add a flat rate of $2.20 for shipping on all orders. We will not ship your order without payment for postage. We do not accept stamps for payment. We have been in business since July 2002."

Comment: Good images. – Mike

Inmate Pen Pal Connection
Attn: Ralph Landi
49 Crown St. 20B
Brooklyn, NY 11225

Pen pal ads, personal webpage, MySpace, Facebook and Craigslist ads. They do it all for one low price. Send 6 stamps for more information.

Inmate Scribes
P.O. Box 371303
Milwaukee, WI 53237

Offers e–mail, facebook, dating sites, pen pal sites, social media, research, friend finding, lyrics and tabs, personal gifts, photo editing, sexy photos and more. Send SASE for a **FREE** brochure.

Inside Out
PO Box 29040
Cleveland, OH 44129

Pen pal services. Write/Send SASE for details.

Website: insideout.com.

JAD Enterprises.
4409 Birdsong
Plano, TX 75093

"100% guaranteed pen pal locator! We have a large database of available men and women seeking prison pen pals. Tell us what you're looking for and we'll make a connection for you. We also offer other services. Sens a SASE for more info!"

Lifeline
63 Forest Rd
Garston, Watford WD25 7QP, UK

International pen pal for death row prisoners only. Waiting list is 3–4 months. Postage for international is 90 cents.

LostVault.com
PO Box 242
Mascot, TN 37806

This is a pen pal website that you can have your family post your profile on for FREE (one ad per inmate!). If you do not have someone on the outside to do it for you, LostVault will do it for $10, or FREE if you are on death row. Fees are to be made payable to LostVault and need to be on a prison–issued check or money order only. Please note that we will not return your photos or send an ad copy if you do not send us a SASE! Photos without a SASE will be held for 30 days and then destroyed.

AD RULES ...

You may not update your ad for free during the 1 year on our website except for address changes, or unless we make an error on your ad. The only exception is for death row inmates, who may update their ad after each 1–year anniversary. If any inmate wants to update the text or photo in his or her ad prior to the 1–year date, the ad will be considered new and the $10 fee will be imposed for a rewritten ad, death row included. If you do not have a photo when your ad is posted and you wish to add one later, no fee will be assessed and the ad will run for the remainder of the 1–year cycle. Bottom line: we don't have time to redo your ad over and over. If you update your ad for any reason, even an error on our part, and wish to have a copy on your new ad, you must include a SASE.

- Your ad must be under 150 words and not contain

sexually explicit or foul language.

- You may send us one photo for your ad. Note that ads with photos are viewed at least 10 times more than those without.
- If you know an inmate who wishes to send us a mail ad, they must send a SASE or stamp for application.
- Please allow 45 days before you inquire about the status of your ad or photo. Mail takes time to get back and forth and to process; ads are placed in the order they are received.

Comment: I'm not sure if you can add more words/photos if you have someone on the outside post your profile, but I plan to check soon. Also, I've seen inmates get hits off this site. —Mike

Meet–An–Inmate
Attn: Arlen Bischke
PO Box 1342
Pendleton, OR 97801

Pen pal service.

Website: meet–an–inmate.com

Pen Pal Project
PO Box 9867
Marian Del Ray, CA 90295

Prison Connection
PO Box 18489
Cleveland Heights, OH 44118

This is a pen pal service. Special – $20 for 2 years. Send SASE for more information.

Prison Inmates Online
8033 W. Sunset Blvd. #7000
Los Angeles, CA 90046

"Prison Inmates Online is much more than a pen pal service. It's your link to the free world during your incarceration! A lot of inmates lose touch with family and friends after being incarcerated. With a PIO profile, friends and family can always find you, see what's going on in your life, and send you a message. Keep your profile updated and never be forgotten. If you find love, don't pull your profile down, just change your relationship status to 'In a Relationship' in your bio and keep your profile going!

Best value for your money: PIO is the best value for your online profile. Why pay more on other websites that only provide less? See how we compare to our competitors with better prices/service.

Profile price and renewals: PIO charges $50 for a profile that includes up to 300 words.

Plus, every time you make a PAID update, your profile is extended for 1 year from the date of the update. Compare that to other websites who charge $40 for a profile that only contains 250 words and renewal rates up to $30 per year.

More photos than anyone else: PIO allows you to submit 5 photos with your profile. Compare that with the 1–2 photos most other services allow you to submit. Additional photos, art and tattoos are 5 for $10. Compare that to other websites that charge you $10 for EACH photo.

Featured Inmate: Our Featured Inmate panel is shown on nearly every page of PIO website and includes a courtesy in the 'ad' space section of the website. Compare that to other services who only show only show featured inmates on the homepage. Become a Featured Inmate for just $30 per month or $180 for the whole year!

Blogs and poems: List a blog or poem on PIO up to 300 words for just $10. Compare that to the $15 other websites charge. Other services like videos, tattoos and documents aren't even provided by other websites.

Documents section: Share documents (legal, stories, journals, diaries) for others to view or download. A great way to inform people who are following you or your case! It's also a rest place to store digital copies of your records in one place. Only $10 for each document title, up to 50 pages.

Tattoo section: Many men and women are drawn to people with tattoos. Why not show off yours in the tattoo section? The photos of your tattoos are linked to your profile page so it's another way to get more visitors to your page. $10 for up to 5 photos.

Videos: YouTube is the Internet's largest video sharing website and is integrated into this site. You can post any video that is listed on YouTube directly to your profile page. Your favorite music video, comedian, or even your own videos if they are posted on YouTube! Only $5 per video!"

Website: prisoninmates.com
Corrlinks:
infoprisoninmates.com

Comment: This may very well be the best profile service I've seen. You can practically have everything a real, personal/company website can have. – Mike

Prison Pen Pals
PO Box 235
East Berlin, PA 17316

Connecting prisoners with pen pals since 1996.

"Our award–winning web site has been seen in 100's of newspapers, dozens of magazines and many TV shows all around the world — Cosmopolitan, The New York Times, The Ricci Lake Show, MSNBC's Homepage and more! We are the most visited, largest and longest running site of its kind on the Internet!

Economy Ad: 1 photo with your name, # and address for a FULL year on the site — $9.95

Basic Ad: Up to 200 words and 1 photo with your name, # and address for a FULL year on the site — $19.95

Gold Star Ad: Up to 300 words and 2 photos with your name, # and address, highlighted with a GOLD STAR and placed on a special list for a FULL year on the site — $39.95

Platinum Ad: Up to 500 words and 5 photos or artwork with your name, # and address, highlighted with LARGE BOLD TEXT and a flashing arrow, placed on the highest traffic area on our site for a FULL year, plus 4 week processing time or 2 **FREE** months — $79.95

Gallery Ad: Up to 500 words and 20 photos or artwork in a fully animated slide show with up to 5 personalized words captioned on each photo, BACKGROUND MUSIC, your name, if and address, highlighted with LARGE BOLD TEXT and a flashing camera, placed on the highest traffic area of our site for a FULL year, plus 4 week processing time or 2 **FREE** months — $99.95

We accept stamps for payment! For a **FREE** brochure/application, send us a SASE today!"

Website: prisonpenpals.com

PrisonerPal.com
PO Box 19689
Houston, TX 77224

Pen Pals for prisoners. Your ad on the Internet, worldwide, only $9.95 for one year. Mail name and address for **FREE** order form.

San Francisco Zen Center
c/o Jeffrey Schnieder
300 Page Street
S.F., CA 94102

This spot provides Buddhist inmates with free–world pen pals.

Comment: The key word is Buddhist. Their "gatekeeper" is Jeffrey Schnider. He's cool, but when I originally wrote he asked me to write an introduction letter, and when he got back at me he told me that I wasn't a real Buddhist so he wasn't going to hook me up, but he would write me a provide me with resources. I had to respect his gangsta. — GURU

Secrets to Prison Pen Pal Success: How to Post FREE Ads on the Internet

This book is by Dupreme Washington and it's $14.95. The ISBN is 978–0–615–36993–8

Comment: I read most of this book and it was really good. My celly has put some of its lessons to use and has received success. — Mike

SexyPrisoners.com

T. Ison (X)
P.O. Box 1445
Flushing, NY 11354

Pen pal site and sexy photo seller. Send SASE for Info.

Tele–pal.com

Tired of waiting on pen pals? Talk to a phone pal! Why write when you can call? We have a phone pal for you and it's more affordable than ever.

Phone Number: (719) 297–1909

WaitingPenPals.com
PO Box 24592
Fort Lauderdale, FL 33307

Send a SASE for information on their pen pal service.

Write4Life
613 Bryden Ave. Ste C #226
Lewiston, ID 83501

"Guaranteed pen pal with write4life! Tell us your interests and we will match you with a pen pal immediately. What are your favorite things to do? What makes you happy? What kind of people intrigue you? We want to know! Write to us and we'll write back! Note: Write4Life provides a guaranteed fictional pen pal with a $10 per month subscription fee. "

Comment: This seems very pathetic and desperate, but maybe it's a PG way of advertising a "freaky letter Service" — like a sexy phone service, but through letters. – Mike

WriteAPrisoner.com
PO Box 10
Edgewater, FL 32132

"We understand the loneliness incarceration can bring... There are other who understand as well. Thousands of people from all walks of life come to our website every day in search of pen pals. They are looking for friendship; they are prepared to offer support; they want to provide encouragement; and they understand the loneliness. If outside companionship could improve your quality of life while incarcerated, join WriteAPrisoner.com. We're dedicated to reducing recidivism. The first step is connecting you with those who understand.

Thousands of people who are interested in corresponding with inmates visit our site each day. Our site is easily accessed from all Internet connected devices including cell phones and is

translated into 51 languages to attract overseas visitors as well. We advertise non–stop on all major search engines and receive millions of page views monthly. We've been seen on MSNBC's Lockup, Dr. Phil, CNN, Women's Entertainment, The Ney York Times, Washington Post, Boston Globe, O Magazine, and many, many more places. Place your pen–pal profile today and start making new friends!"

A one year profile (250 words and 1 picture) is $40. You can add an additional photo or piece of artwork for $10 each. Each additional 50 words is $5. You can add a bio entry for $15 (250 words). Each additional 50 words is $5. You can pay for your profile via institutional check, money order or credit card. If you'd like to pay with postage stamps, request their Stamp Payment Guidelines/Prices first by sending them a SASE. For a **FREE** copy of their brochure with all the profile details, send SASE.

WriteAPrisoner.com Stamp Guidelines/Prices

"When we accept stamps as payment, it prohibits us from utilizing lower bulk mail rates; therefore, prices are slightly higher when paying with stamps. The prices and rules are as follows:

1. Stamps must be on sheets or rolls. No more than 10 individual stamps can be accepted.
2. Stamps must not be taped, stapled or adhered together.

Writesomeoneinprison.com; Nubian Princess Ent.
POB 37
Timmonsville, SC 29161

This is a good pen pal service. They accept stamps. Send SASE for more information.

Writetoinmates.com
5729 Main St., # 362
Springfield, OR 97478

Pen pal website3. Stamps must be an acceptable form of payment from your institution. If your institution prohibits using stamps as currency, we cannot accept them from you.

4. Only Forever stamps can be used as payment.

5. Stamps will not be accepted if they are removed from their original sheets and placed on new ones.

Profile Price List in Stamps...

Standard one year profile: 115 Forever stamps.
Additional photo/artwork: 30 Forever stamps.
Additional words: 15 Forever stamps for each additional 50 words.
Text change: 30 Forever stamps.
Photo change: 30 Forever stamps for 1 photo.
Additional photo/artwork: 30 Forever stamps.
Additional words: 15 Forever stamps for each additional 50 words.
Standard profile renewal: 90 Forever stamps.
Blogs: 45 Forever stamps for 1 250 word blog.
Poetry: 45 Forever stamps for 250 words.

Send SASE and request 'Stamp Payment Guidelines' for further details."

Writeaprisoner.com
P.O. Box 10
Edgewater, FL 32132

This is one of the best pen–pal websites they also offer a **FREE** reintegration profile. Send SASE for **FREE** application.

THE CELL BLOCK

MIKE ENEMIGO is the new prison/street art sensation who has written and published several books. He is inspired by emotion; hope; pain; dreams and nightmares. He physically lives somewhere in a California prison cell where he works relentlessly creating his next piece. His mind and soul are elsewhere; seeing, studying, learning, and drawing inspiration to tear down suppressive walls and inspire the culture by pushing artistic boundaries.

THE CELL BLOCK is an independent multimedia company with the objective of accurately conveying the prison/street experience with the credibility and honesty that only one who has lived it can deliver, through literature and other arts, and to entertain and enlighten while doing so. Everything published by The Cell Block has been created by a prisoner, while in a prison cell.

THE BEST RESOURCE DIRECTORY FOR PRISONERS, $17.95 & $5.00 S/H: This book has over 1,450 resources for prisoners! Includes: Pen–Pal Companies! Non–Nude Photo Sellers! Free Books and Other Publications! Legal Assistance! Prisoner Advocates! Prisoner Assistants! Correspondence Education! Money–Making Opportunities! Resources for Prison Writers, Poets, Artists! And much, much more! Anything you can think of doing from your prison cell, this book contains the resources to do it!

A GUIDE TO RELAPSE PREVENTION FOR PRISONERS, $15.00 & $5.00 S/H: This book provides the information and guidance that can make a real difference in the preparation of a comprehensive relapse prevention plan. Discover how to meet the parole board's expectation using these proven and practical principles. Included is a blank template and sample relapse prevention plan to assist in your preparation.

THEE ENEMY OF THE STATE (SPECIAL EDITION), $9.99 & $4.00 S/H: Experience the inspirational journey of a kid who was introduced to the art of rapping in 1993, struggled between his dream of becoming a professional rapper and the reality of the streets, and was finally offered a recording deal in 1999, only to be arrested minutes later and eventually sentenced to life in prison for murder... However, despite his harsh reality, he dedicated himself to hip–hop once again, and with resilience and determination, he sets out to prove he may just be one of the dopest rhyme writers/spitters ever .... At this point, it becomes deeper than rap .... Welcome to a preview of the greatest story you never heard.

LOST ANGELS: $15.00 & $5.00: David Rodrigo was a child who belonged to no world; rejected for his mixed heritage by most of his family and raised by an outcast uncle in the mean streets of East L.A. Chance cast him into a far darker and more devious pit of intrigue that stretched from the barest gutters to the halls of power in the great city. Now, to survive the clash of lethal forces arrayed about him, and to protect those he loves, he has only two allies; his quick wits, and the flashing blade that earned young David the street name, Viper.

LOYALTY AND BETRAYAL DELUXE EDITION, $19.99 & $7.00 S/H: Chunky was an associate of and soldier for the notorious Mexican Mafia – La Eme. That is, of course, until he was betrayed by those, he was most loyal to. Then he vowed to become their worst enemy. And though they've attempted to kill him numerous times, he still to this day is running around making a mockery of their organization .... This is the story of how it all began.

MONEY IZ THE MOTIVE: SPECIAL 2–IN–1 EDITION, $19.99 & $7.00 S/H: Like most kids growing up in the hood, Kano has a dream of going from rags to riches. But when his plan to get fast money by robbing the local "mom and pop" shop goes wrong, he quickly finds himself sentenced to serious prison time. Follow Kano as he is schooled to the ways of the game by some of the most respected OGs whoever did it; then is set free and given the resources to put his schooling into action and build the ultimate hood empire...

DEVILS & DEMONS: PART 1, $15.00 & $5.00 S/H: When Talton leaves the West Coast to set up shop in Florida he meets the female version of himself: A drug dealing murderess with psychological issues. A whirlwind of sex, money and murder inevitably ensues and Talton finds himself on the run from the law with nowhere to turn to. When his team from home finds out he's in trouble, they get on a plane heading south...

DEVILS & DEMONS: PART 2, $15.00 & $5.00 S/H: The Game is bitter–sweet for Talton, aka Gangsta. The same West Coast Clique who came to his aid ended up putting bullets into the chest of the woman he had fallen in love with. After leaving his ride or die in a puddle of her own blood, Talton finds himself on a flight back to Oak Park, the neighborhood where it all started...

DEVILS & DEMONS: PART 3, $15.00 & $5.00 S/H: Talton is on the road to retribution for the murder of the love of his life. Dante and his crew of killers are on a path of no return. This urban classic is based on real–life West Coast underworld politics. See what happens when a group of YG's find themselves in the midst of real underworld demons...

DEVILS & DEMONS: PART 4, $15.00 & $5.00 S/H: After waking up from a coma, Alize has locked herself away from the rest of the world. When her sister Brittany and their friend finally take her on a girl's night out, she meets Luck – a drug dealing womanizer.

FREAKY TALES, $15.00 & $5.00 S/H: Freaky Tales is the first book in a brand–new erotic series. King Guru, author of the *Devils & Demons* books, has put together a collection of sexy short stories and memoirs. In true TCB fashion, all of the erotic tales included in this book have been loosely based on true accounts told to, or experienced by the author.

THE ART & POWER OF LETTER WRITING FOR PRISONERS: DELUXE EDITION $19.99 & $7.00 S/H: When locked inside a prison cell, being able to write well is the most powerful skill you can have! Learn how to increase your power by writing high–quality personal and formal letters! Includes letter templates, pen–pal website strategies, punctuation guide and more!

THE PRISON MANUAL: $24.99 & $7.00 S/H: *The Prison Manual* is your all–in–one book on how to not only survive the rough terrain of the American prison system, but use it to your advantage so you can THRIVE from it! How to Use Your Prison Time to YOUR Advantage; How to Write Letters that Will Give You Maximum Effectiveness; Workout and Physical Health Secrets that Will Keep You as FIT as Possible; The Psychological impact of incarceration and How to Maintain Your MAXIMUM Level of Mental Health; Prison Art Techniques; Fulfilling Food Recipes; Parole Preparation Strategies and much, MUCH more!

GET OUT, STAY OUT!, $16.95 & $5.00 S/H: This book should be in the hands of everyone in a prison cell. It reveals a challenging but clear course for overcoming the obstacles that stand between prisoners and their freedom. For those behind bars, one goal outshines all others: GETTING OUT! After being released, that goal then shifts to STAYING OUT! This book will help prisoners do both. It has been masterfully constructed into five parts that will help prisoners maximize focus while they strive to accomplish whichever goal is at hand.

MOB$TAR MONEY, $12.00 & $4.00 S/H: After Trey's mother is sent to prison for 75 years to life, he and his little brother are moved from their home in Sacramento, California, to his grandmother's house in Stockton, California where he is forced to find his way in life and become a man on his own in the city's grimy streets. One day, on his way home from the local corner store, Trey has a rough encounter with the neighborhood bully. Luckily, that's when Tyson, a member of the MOBTAR, a local "get money" gang comes to his aid. The two kids quickly become friends, and it doesn't take long before Trey is embraced into the notorious MOB$TAR money gang, which opens the door to an adventure full of sex, money, murder and mayhem that will change his life forever... You will never guess how this story ends!

BLOCK MONEY, $12.00 & $4.00 S/H: Beast, a young thug from the grimy streets of central Stockton, California lives The Block; breathes The Block; and has committed himself to bleed The Block for all it's worth until his very last breath. Then, one day, he meets Nadia; a stripper at the local club who piques his curiosity with her beauty, quick–witted intellect and rider qualities. The problem? She has a man – Esco – a local kingpin with money and power. It doesn't take long, however, before a devious plot is hatched to pull off a heist worth an indeterminable amount of money. Following the acts of treachery, deception and betrayal are twists and turns and a bloody war that will leave you speechless!

HOW TO HUSTLE AND WIN: SEX, MONEY, MURDER EDITION $15.00 & $5.00 S/H: *How To Hu$tle and Win: Sex, Money, Murder Edition* is the grittiest, underground self–help manual for the 21st century street entrepreneur in print. Never has there been such a book written for today's gangsters, goons and go–getters. This self–help handbook is an absolute must–have for anyone who is actively connected to the streets.

RAW LAW: YOUR RIGHTS, & HOW TO SUE WHEN THEY ARE VIOLATED! $15.00 & $5.00 S/H: *Raw Law For Prisoners* is a clear and concise guide for prisoners and their advocates to understanding civil rights laws guaranteed to prisoners under the US Constitution, and how to successfully file a lawsuit when those rights have been violated! From initial complaint to trial, this book will take you through the entire process, step by step, in simple, easy–to–understand terms. Also included are several examples where prisoners have sued prison officials successfully, resulting in changes of unjust rules and regulations and recourse for rights violations, oftentimes resulting in rewards of thousands, even millions of dollars in damages! If you feel your rights have been violated, don't lash out at guards, which is usually ineffective and only makes matters worse. Instead, defend yourself successfully by using the legal system, and getting the power of the courts on your side!

HOW TO WRITE URBAN BOOKS FOR MONEY & FAME: $16.95 & $5.00 S/H: Inside this book you will learn the true story of how Mike Enemigo and King Guru have received money and fame from inside their prison cells by writing urban books; the secrets to writing hood classics so you, too, can be caked up and famous; proper punctuation using hood examples; and resources you can use to achieve your money motivated ambitions! If you're a prisoner who want to write urban novels for money and fame, this must–have manual will give you all the game!

PRETTY GIRLS LOVE BAD BOYS: AN INMATE'S GUIDE TO GETTING GIRLS: $15.00 & $5.00 S/H: Tired of the same, boring, cliché pen pal books that don't tell you what you really need to know? If so, this book is for you! Anything you need to know on the art of long and short distance seduction is included within these pages! Not only does it give you the science of attracting pen pals from websites, it also includes psychological profiles and instructions on how to seduce any woman you set your sights on! Includes interviews of women who have fallen in love with prisoners, bios for pen pal ads, pre–written love letters, romantic poems, love–song lyrics, jokes and much, much more!

This book is the ultimate guide – a must–have for any prisoner who refuses to let prison walls affect their MAC'n.

THE LADIES WHO LOVE PRISONERS, $15.00 & $5.00 S/H: New Special Report reveals the secrets of real women who have fallen in love with prisoners, regardless of crime, sentence, or location. This info will give you a HUGE advantage in getting girls from prison.

THE MILLIONAIRE PRISONER: PART 1, $16.95 & $5.00 S/H

THE MILLIONAIRE PRISONER: PART 2, $16.95 & $5.00 S/H

THE MILLIONAIRE PRISONER: SPECIAL 2–IN–1 EDITION, $24.99 & $7.00 S/H: Why wait until you get out of prison to achieve your dreams? Here's a blueprint that you can use to become successful! *The Millionaire Prisoner* is your complete reference to overcoming any obstacle in prison. You won't be able to put it down! With this book you will discover the secrets to: Making money from your cell! Obtain FREE money for correspondence courses! Become an expert on any topic! Develop the habits of the rich! Network with celebrities! Set up your own website! Market your products, ideas and services! Successfully use prison pen pal websites! All of this and much, much more! This book has enabled thousands of prisoners to succeed and it will show you the way also!

THE MILLIONAIRE PRISONER 3: SUCCESS UNIVERSITY, $16.95 & $5 S/H: Why wait until you get out of prison to achieve your dreams? Here's a new–look blueprint that you can use to be successful! *The Millionaire Prisoner 3* contains advanced strategies to overcoming any obstacle in prison. You won't be able to put it down!

THE MILLIONAIRE PRISONER 4: PEN PAL MASTERY, $16.95 & $5.00 S/H: Tired of subpar results? Here's a master blueprint that you can use to get tons of pen pals! *TMP 4: Pen Pal Mastery* is your complete roadmap to finding your one true love. You won't be able to put it down! With this book you'll DISCOVER the SECRETS to: Get FREE pen pals & which sites are best to use; Successful tactics female prisoners can win with; Use astrology to find love; friendship & more; Build a winning social media presence; Playing phone tag & successful sex talk; Hidden benefits of foreign pen pals; Find your success mentors; Turning "hits" into friendships; Learn how to write letters/emails that get results. All of this and much more!

GET OUT, GET RICH: HOW TO GET PAID LEGALLY WHEN YOU GET OUT OF PRISON!, $16.95 & $5.00 S/H: Many of you are incarcerated for a money–motivated crime. But w/ today's tech & opportunities, not only is the crime–for–money risk/reward ratio not strategically wise, it's not even necessary. You can earn much more money by partaking in any one of the easy, legal hustles explained in this book, regardless of your record. Help yourself earn an honest income so you can not only make a lot of money, but say good–bye to penitentiary chances and prison forever! (Note: Many things in this book can even he done from inside prison.) (ALSO PUBLISHED AS *HOOD MILLIONAIRE: HOW TO HUSTLE AND WIN LEGALLY!*)

THE CEO MANUAL: HOW TO START A BUSINESS WHEN YOU GET OUT OF PRISON, $16.95 & $5.00 S/H: $16.95 & $5 S/H: This new book will teach you the simplest way to start your own business when you get out of prison. Includes: Start–up Steps! The Secrets to Pulling Money from Investors! How to Manage People Effectively! How To Legally Protect Your Assets from "them"! Hundreds of resources to get you started, including a list of "loan friendly" banks! (ALSO PUBLISHED AS *CEO MANUAL: START A BUSINESS, BE A BOSS!*)

THE MONEY MANUAL: UNDERGROUND CASH SECRETS EXPOSED! 16.95 & $5.00 S/H: Becoming a millionaire is equal parts what you make, and what you don't spend – AKA save. All Millionaires and Billionaires have mastered the art of not only making money, but keeping the money they make (remember Donald Trump's tax maneuvers?), as well as establishing credit so that they are loaned money by banks and trusted with money from investors: AKA OPM – other people's money. And did you know there are millionaires and billionaires just waiting to GIVE money away? It's true! These are all very–little known secrets "they" don't want YOU to know about, but that I'm exposing in my new book!

HOOD MILLIONAIRE; HOW TO HUSTLE & WIN LEGALLY, $16.95 & $5.00 S/H: Hustlin' is a way of life in the hood. We all have money motivated ambitions, not only because we gotta eat, but because status is oftentimes determined by one's own salary. To achieve what we consider financial success, we often invest our efforts into illicit activities – we take penitentiary chances. This leads to a life in and out of prison, sometimes death – both of which are counterproductive to gettin' money. But there's a solution to this, and I have it...

CEO MANUAL: START A BUSINESS BE A BOSS, $16.95 & $5.00 S/H: After the success of the urban–entrepreneur classic *Hood Millionaire: How To Hustle & Win Legally!*, self–made millionaires Mike Enemigo and Sav Hustle team back up to bring you the latest edition of the Hood Millionaire series – *CEO Manual: Start A Business, Be A Boss!* In this latest collection of game laying down the art of "hoodpreneurship", you will learn such things as: 5 Core Steps to Starting Your Own Business! 5 Common Launch Errors You Must Avoid! How To Write a Business Plan! How To Legally Protect Your Assets From "Them"! How To Make Your Business Fundable, Where to Get Money for Your Start–up Business, and even How to Start a Business With No Money! You will learn How to Drive

Customers to Your Website, How to Maximize Marketing Dollars, Contract Secrets for the savvy boss, and much, much more! And as an added bonus, we have included over 200 Business Resources, from government agencies and small business development centers, to a secret list of small–business friendly banks that will help you get started!

PAID IN FULL: WELCOME TO DA GAME, $15.00 & $5.00 S/H. In 1983, the movie *Scarface* inspired many kids growing up in America's inner cities to turn their rags into riches by becoming cocaine kingpins. Harlem's Azie Faison was one of them. Faison would ultimately connect with Harlem's Rich Porter and Alpo Martinez, and the trio would go on to become certified street legends of the '80s and early '90s. Years later, Dame Dash and Roc–A–Fella Films would tell their story in the based–on–actual–events movie, *Paid in Full*. But now, we are telling the story our way – The Cell Block way – where you will get a perspective of the story that the movie did not show, ultimately learning an outcome that you did not expect. Book one of our series, *Paid in Full: Welcome to da Game*, will give you an inside look at a key player in this story, one that is not often talked about – Lulu, the Columbian cocaine kingpin with direct ties to Pablo Escobar, who plugged Azie in with an unlimited amount of top–tier cocaine at dirt–cheap prices that helped boost the trio to neighborhood superstars and certified kingpin status... until greed, betrayal, and murder destroyed everything....

OJ'S LIFE BEHIND BARS, $15.00 & $5 S/H: In 1994, Heisman Trophy winner and NFL superstar OJ Simpson was arrested for the brutal murder of his ex–wife Nicole Brown–Simpson and her friend Ron Goldman. In 1995, after the "trial of the century," he was acquitted of both murders, though most of the world believes he did it. In 2007 OJ was again arrested, but this time in Las Vegas, for armed robbery and kidnapping. On October 3, 2008 he was found guilty sentenced to 33 years and was sent to Lovelock Correctional Facility, in Lovelock, Nevada.

There he met inmate–author Vernon Nelson. Vernon was granted a true, insider's perspective into the mind and life of one of the country's most notorious men; one that has never been provided…until now.

BLINDED BY BETRAYAL, $15.00 & $5.00 S/H. Khalil wanted nothing more than to chase his rap dream when he got out of prison. After all, a fellow inmate had connected him with a major record producer that could help him take his career to unimaginable heights, and his girl is in full support of his desire to trade in his gun for a mic. Problem is, Khalil's crew, the notorious Blood Money Squad, awaited him with open arms, unaware of his desire to leave the game alone, and expected him to jump head first into the life of fast money and murder. Will Khalil be able to balance his desire to get out of the game with the expectations of his gang to participate in it? Will he be able to pull away before it's too late? Or, will the streets pull him right back in, ultimately causing his demise? One thing for sure, the streets are loyal to no one, and blood money comes with bloody consequences....

THE MOB, $16.99 & $5 S/H. PaperBoy is a Bay Area boss who has invested blood, sweat, and years into building The Mob – a network of Bay Area Street legends, block bleeders, and underground rappers who collaborate nationwide in the interest of pushing a multi–million–dollar criminal enterprise of sex, drugs, and murder.

AOB, $15.00 & $5 S/H. Growing up in the Bay Area, Manny Fresh the Best had a front–row seat to some of the coldest players to ever do it. And you already know, A.O.B. is the name of the Game! So, When Manny Fresh slides through Stockton one day and sees Rosa, a stupid–bad Mexican chick with a whole lotta 'talent' behind her walking down the street tryna get some money, he knew immediately what he had to do: Put it In My Pocket!

AOB 2, $15.00 & $5 S/H.

AOB 3, $15.00 & $5 S/H

PIMPOLOGY: THE 7 ISMS OF THE GAME, $15.00 & $5 S/H: It's been said that if you knew better, you'd do better. So, in the spirit of dropping jewels upon the rare few who truly want to know how to win, this collection of exclusive Game has been compiled. And though a lot of so–called players claim to know how the Pimp Game is supposed to go, none have revealed the real. . . Until now!

JAILHOUSE PUBLISHING FOR MONEY, POWER & FAME: $24.99 & $7 S/H: In 2010, after flirting with the idea for two years, Mike Enemigo started writing his first book. In 2014, he officially launched his publishing company, The Cell Block, with the release of five books. Of course, with no mentor(s), how–to guides, or any real resources, he was met with failure after failure as he tried to navigate the treacherous goal of publishing books from his prison cell. However, he was determined to make it. He was determined to figure it out and he refused to quit. In Mike's new book, *Jailhouse Publishing for Money, Power, and Fame,* he breaks down all his jailhouse publishing secrets and strategies, so you can do all he's done, but without the trials and tribulations he's had to go through...

KITTY KAT, ADULT ENTERTAINMENT RESOURCE BOOK, $24.99 & $7.00 S/H: This book is jam packed with hundreds of sexy non nude photos including photo spreads. The book contains the complete info on sexy photo sellers, hot magazines, page turning bookstore, sections on strip clubs, porn stars, alluring models, thought provoking stories and must–see movies.

PRISON LEGAL GUIDE, $24.99 & $7.00 S/H: The laws of the U.S. Judicial system are complex, complicated, and always growing and changing. Many prisoners spend days on end digging through its intricacies. Pile on top of the legal code the rules and regulations of a correctional facility, and you can see how high the deck is being stacked against you. Correct legal information is the key to your survival when you have run afoul of the system (or it is running afoul of you). Whether you are an accomplished jailhouse lawyer helping newbies learn the ropes, an old head fighting bare–knuckle for your rights in the courts, or a hustler just looking to beat the latest write–up – this book has something for you!

PRISON HEALTH HANDBOOK, $19.99 & $7.00 S/H: The Prison Health Handbook is your one–stop go–to source for information on how to maintain your best health while inside the American prison system. Filled with information, tips, and secrets from doctors, gurus, and other experts, this book will educate you on such things as proper workout and exercise regimens; yoga benefits for prisoners; how to meditate effectively; pain management tips; sensible dieting solutions; nutritional knowledge; an understanding of various cancers, diabetes, hepatitis, and other diseases all too common in prison; how to effectively deal with mental health issues such as stress, PTSD, anxiety, and depression; a list of things your doctors DON'T want YOU to know; and much, much more!

All books are available on thecellblock.net.

You can also order by sending a money order or institutional check to:

The Cell Block
PO Box 1025
Rancho Cordova, CA 95741

Made in United States
Troutdale, OR
11/05/2024

24457071R00136